Golnaz Hashemzadeh Bonde was born in Iran in 1983 and fled with her parents to Sweden as a young child. She graduated from the Stockholm School of Economics was named one of fifty Goldman Sachs Global Leaders. She is the founder ... or of Inkludera Invest, a non-prof... ting marginalization in society ... who have developed pragmatic s...

D0533393

Hashemzadeh Bonde lives ... her husband and daughter.

'*What We Owe* refuses sentimental consolations ... Terse, urgent prose – ably channelled by Elizabeth Clark Wessel, the translator-gives pace and heft to a novel of contagious trauma. Still, Ms Hashemzadeh Bonde lets in a closing ray of hope' *The Economist*

'A haunting and emotional tale of survival, of what it means to be a refugee' *Literary Review*

'I read this ferocious novel in one sitting, enthralled by the rage of its narrator. Nahid confronts her own suffering with dark humor and noisy honesty, while taking aim at a patriarchal tradition that expects her to be silent' Leni Zumas, author of *Red Clocks*

'A short yet remarkable novel ... Rather than a gentle meditation on a life lived to the full, *What We Owe* is filled with the rage of a woman who has been through trauma and loss, who has been left haunted by violence, and who wants more from those that love her' *Stylist*

'Translated – gorgeously and simply – by Wessel, Nahid's sentences are short and thrillingly brutal, and the result is exhilarating. Hashemzadeh Bonde, unafraid of ugliness and seemingly unconcerned with likability, has produced a startling meditation on death, national identity, and motherhood. Always arresti... not without hope'...

What We Owe

GOLNAZ HASHEMZADEH BONDE

Translated by Elizabeth Clark Wessel

FLEET
2019

FLEET

First published in Sweden in 2017 by Wahlström & Widstrand as *Det var vi*
First published in Great Britain in 2018 by Fleet
This paperback edition published in 2019 by Fleet

1 3 5 7 9 10 8 6 4 2

Copyright © Golnaz Hashemzadeh Bonde 2017
Translation copyright © Elizabeth Clark Wessel 2018

The moral right of the author has been asserted.

All characters and events in this publication, other than those clearly in the public domain, are fictitious and any resemblance to real persons, living or dead, is purely coincidental.

All rights reserved.
No part of this publication may be reproduced, stored in a retrieval system, or transmitted, in any form or by any means, without the prior permission in writing of the publisher, nor be otherwise circulated in any form of binding or cover other than that in which it is published and without a similar condition including this condition being imposed on the subsequent purchaser.

A CIP catalogue record for this book is available from the British Library.

The cost of this translation was defrayed by a subsidy from the Swedish Arts Council, gratefully acknowledged.

ISBN 978-0-7088-9882-6

Typeset in Sabon by M Rules
Printed and bound in Great Britain by Clays Ltd, Elcograf S.p.A.

Papers used by Fleet are from well-managed forests and other responsible sources.

Fleet
An imprint of
Little, Brown Book Group
Carmelite House
50 Victoria Embankment
London EC4Y 0DZ

An Hachette UK Company
www.hachette.co.uk

www.littlebrown.co.uk

For Noor Koriander

My mother said: if you could regard
the circumstances as extenuating you
would let me off easier.

Athena Farrokhzad,
trans. Jen Hayashida

I've always carried my death with me. Perhaps saying so is trite, an observation the dying always make. But I'm not like other people, in this as in everything else, or so I like to believe. And I do believe it, truly. I said as much when Masood died. Our time was always borrowed. We weren't supposed to be alive. We should have died in the revolution. In its aftermath. In the war. But I was given some thirty more years. Over half my life. It's a considerable length of time, something to be grateful for. The same length as my daughter's life. Yes, that's one way to see it. I was allowed to create her. But she didn't need me that long. No one did. You think because you're a parent, you're needed. It's not true. People find a way to get by. Who says I was worth more than the trouble I caused. I don't believe it. I'm not the type who gives more than I take. I should be. I'm a mother after all. It's my job to bear the weight, bear it for others. But I never have, not for anyone.

'You have at most six months left to live,' the fucking witch says to me. She says it like she's delivering some trivial but unfortunate news. In the same tone of voice the daycare teacher used to tell me that someone had hit Aram. A little bit sad. A little bit guilty. And the witch doesn't even look at me while she says it, just stares into her computer screen. As if that contains the truth. As if the screen were the one being harmed. Then the tears start running down her cheeks, and she stares down at her lap. Now she's the victim. She needs comfort.

Shut up! I want to scream. Who are you to tell me I'm going to die. Who are you to weep, as if my life has anything to do with you. But I don't scream. Not this time. I surprise myself.

'I want to speak to your supervisor,' I say instead.

She seems taken aback. Probably thinks that was the wrong reaction. Thinks I should be weeping, too.

'I know this is hard . . . hard to hear. But it doesn't matter who you talk to,' she says. 'The CT scan, the test results. They're indisputable. You have cancer. And it's . . . it's quite advanced.'

She falls silent and looks at me. Waiting for my face to confirm that I understand. But it doesn't, so she continues.

'It's stage four. Cancer. That means you don't have much time.'

'Shut up!' Now I do say it. 'I'm a nurse. I've worked in health care for twenty-five years. I know you're not allowed to say that to me. You have no idea how long I have left. You're not God!'

She backs away in her chair, upset. She must be in her thirties, with her hair held high in two childish pigtails. A photo of a baby stands on her desktop. I shake my head. She has no clue what she knows or doesn't know.

We sit in silence, until she wipes her tears onto her sleeve and leaves. I sit frozen for a moment then reach for my handbag and take out my phone. I should call someone. I should call my daughter. Say: *Hello, my cursed little crow. Now your mother is going to die, too.*

Damn. I try to write a text message to Zahra instead. But I erase it. What do you say? *Hello friend, so much struggle, and now it's over.* I can't.

I hear two voices approaching, the doctor and her supervisor. They stop outside the door. Whispering. It's obvious they don't face death often here at this GP clinic. They're discussing who should go inside and talk to me. I understand. They want to get on with their day. Move on to the next patient. Not fall behind. The last thing they want to do is take shit from some dying woman. I consider my options. Should I just pack up and go? Spare them. Spare myself. I grab my coat. It's red. I reach for my handbag. Also red. I look down at my boots. Red. All the banalities I care about. Cared about. My hands start to shake, then my shoulders. I drop my handbag onto the floor. Trying to hold back the sob rising in my body. At that very moment, they open the door. Step inside. Look at me. I see how they'd like to turn and go. I don't want to scare them. I try to smile. But it washes over me. What they don't know. What nobody in this fucking country knows, although they know so much. About pain and loss and struggle. I start to cry. I cry, and I cry. She cries too, the first doctor. Poor thing. She thinks she has something to cry about.

Still she apologises. The older doctor. Says they have no idea how long I'll live. Could be a few weeks, or a few years.

'But you will die from this cancer,' she says. 'It's best you're open about it, tell your nearest and dearest. Especially your children . . .'

You tell my child, I think. But I must not say it out loud, because she continues.

'It will be difficult of course. Being honest with your children can be very difficult. But they deserve to know. They need to prepare themselves.'

I look questioningly at her. She doesn't understand what I'm wondering, but I assume she knows there's no other way I can look at her.

'Masood's just died . . . her father. He died very recently,' I say.

She nods.

'He died suddenly. Don't you think that's better? For Aram, for my daughter? Than having to live with this death. Wait for it. Wouldn't it be better if I just up and die one day?'

'I don't know,' she says. As if I were expecting a real answer. 'But you're going to need your daughter. This won't be easy.'

She holds out a brochure. How to prepare for death, or something like that. I shake my head.

'I'm not going to die! I'm going to fight. I want to start treatment right away!'

She hesitates.

'Yes, we're referring you to an oncologist. But you'll have to wait a bit to get in. It's the Easter holiday soon. It may take a while before you're in treatment, Nahid.'

I lean forward in my chair.

'But you told me I'm going to die. I'll die if we do nothing. This is an emergency!'

She shakes her head.

'Cancer is not an emergency. A few weeks won't matter, Nahid.'

'What do you mean, what is it if it's not an emergency?'

'Well, cancer is considered a chronic disease.'

I raise my eyebrows.

'Chronic? How can it be chronic if I'm going to die soon?'

'I'm sorry.'

She leans against the doorjamb. She hasn't even stepped into the room. She stopped there, on the other side of the room. As if it were contagious. Cancer. Death.

'I'm sorry.'

I stand up.

'Don't apologise. I'm not dead yet.'

I pull out my lipstick and apply it to my lips. Show her I'm strong. Then I leave. Walk right past her. They call after me, but I walk on. Hurrying, hurrying to keep myself from turning around and throwing myself into her arms to beg for comfort. Beg for sincere promises and solace.

Only when I get home do I see the mascara running down my face. The lipstick smeared outside the edges of my lips. I look frightening. Like I'm the witch. A scarecrow. A dummy. A dead person. Someone who has no idea what it's like to be alive.

I have six months left to live. Or a few weeks. Or a few years. I sit down on the sofa without washing my face. Just sit there with my hands in my lap wondering what to do now. What do you do when they tell you you're dying?

Baskets of paper stand on the rug. They've been there for months, maybe years. I've always supposed if I leave them out I'll finally get around to sorting through them. Dealing with them. Perhaps that's what I should do now. Go through my papers. Make sure everything's in order. Old phone bills. Account statements. Tax forms. It occurs to me there was never any reason for those baskets after all. Everything can be thrown away. Might as well toss it all.

Aram can do it. Later. Afterwards.

I pick up a notebook and pen from the table. Start scribbling. Realise all my notes are in those baskets, too. Maybe I should throw at least the notes away. What will she think if she reads them. She'll find out how lonely I was. How angry I was. I should want to protect her, but I don't. Let her! Let her feel my pain. I know it's wrong, that my maternal instincts should tell me otherwise. But they don't, so I let it be.

My pen scratches across the paper. I want to know what I'm leaving behind. When I divorced Masood, he took it all. I didn't get anything. I've been collecting ever since.

Accumulating, building. Building up my security. My future. And now there isn't one. I laugh out loud. There is no future. Think if people knew. You put so much time into planning for the future, and then it doesn't even exist. Who would have thought.

Would I have lived differently if I'd known? Skipped all those back-to-back shifts? Lived on credit cards, left behind huge debts? I'm not sure. Maybe. Probably. I mean, why not. What would have stopped me?

I write it all down. The apartment I live in. The gold jewellery in my safe deposit box. Those damn Telia shares they tricked us into buying. The money in my savings account. The emergency stash in the closet. I write it all down, count it up. It adds up to a lot. A lot of money!

First I think, that's a lot of money for somebody like me. But then, no, that's wrong. There are plenty of people who were born here, who grew up in this country, who don't, can't, couldn't gather that kind of money. They're too comfortable, too lazy. They don't have what I have. They've left nothing behind.

It's not just a lot of money for somebody like me. It's a lot of money. A lot of money for Aram. If she doesn't think so, she can shove it! A war baby. She should be grateful. She will be grateful, I know that. The money will do her more good than me. She has more of a chance to live, to be alive. Not just because I'm dying. But because I never had it. The ability to just live. What I was born with, born into, was the ability to survive. I grew up to survive. That's not the same as living. I don't know if my daughter has the ability to survive. Maybe, she was almost born in an air-raid shelter. But not her friends. Not children born in Sweden.

That reminds me of the doctor at the clinic. And her tears. What does *she* have to cry about?

My mother was married off when she was nine years old. It's difficult for me to even say those words. I'm ashamed of them. It's like I'm condoning it just by mentioning it. So I don't. She was nine years old, and my father was twenty-seven. That wasn't unusual, back then. But I don't think the fact that it was ordinary made any difference to her. That it affected what it felt like for her to be forced to leave her parents and start a sexual relationship with an unknown adult man.

I can't be angry with my father, he did what one did. But I think of that little girl, who she was, and the thought of her evokes more maternal feelings from me than I've had even for my own child. I think of that girl, how if I could have saved her, I'd have also saved myself. If I could save her, I could save my daughter, too.

My mother was twelve when she gave birth to Maryam. My heart bleeds for both of them. A twelve-year-old with a baby in her arms. A baby with a twelve-year-old as her fixed point in the world. I don't know what happened inside her. But I think she shut down. I think that's the only thing you can do. A twelve-year-old with a baby in her arms. What good could we do her?

She ended up on her own young. When my father died, she

was only thirty-seven years old and the mother of seven. It made no practical difference that he disappeared.

He'd been ill for a long time. Maybe he was just another child to her. I don't know. She didn't talk about him. She didn't talk about men. In all our wedding photos, she holds herself up straight, the proud mother of the bride, but she never smiles. Men and marriage were a necessary evil in her eyes. Or maybe not even necessary, maybe just unavoidable shit.

My mother. How she suffered during the revolution. You would think that a woman who'd given birth to seven daughters might get some peace of mind. No sons to send to war. No sons to mourn. But it was the wrong decade, or we were the wrong kind of women. We fought in the streets, while she sat up at night. Waiting, pacing, weeping.

A few weeks. Half a year. A few years. Does it make a difference? I'm not sure. They are different amounts of time. I understand that. But what difference does time make at this point? What will I do with time? Sick time. Alone time. Time spent waiting to die. What do you do with time, if you're not building a future? I don't know. And I think that might be why. Maybe that's why this is happening to me, maybe that's why the cancer chose me. Because I don't know what to do with time. Because I don't know what to do with life.

I can't stand it, not that thought.

I get up and grab my phone. Dial a number. It's the only number I can call.

'*Allo!?*'

I see her in front of me. See her sink down on the stool by her landline, sighing deeply before picking it up. She expects bad news. She prepares for it in self-defence.

'*Salam, maman.*' I swallow hard, trying to push down what's welling up.

'Nahid? Nahid, is that you? Has something happened, is everything all right?'

'Everything's fine. Very good. I . . . I just miss you.'

'That's life, Nahid. That's life.'

We both fall silent for a moment, then she starts telling me the usual. About her neighbours, the price of tomatoes, her rheumatism. I listen. It's a conversation exactly like the one we had last week. Just like all our conversations. A conversation that is completely unaffected by this particular day, except I press a pillow to my face to stifle the sound of myself.

'Nahid, are you still there?'

I know my voice won't hold so I hang up. She'll think that the call was dropped, like so many of our calls have been dropped over the years. Next time I call, it'll be forgotten.

It's getting dark by the time I finally pick up the phone again. I don't know how I chose whom to call, why I call Zahra. But I do, and it's such a relief. Such a relief to tell somebody, to hear another human being weep. I'm glad it makes her sad. Glad she'll miss me. It feels good to hear somebody react the way they're supposed to. To know you can react like this. I listen quietly for a bit while she weeps, then I start to comfort her.

'It's OK,' I say. 'I haven't had a bad life.'

We fall silent. We don't know if that's true. But we don't say anything to the contrary. We just listen to each other's silence, and that's enough.

'Have you told Aram?' she asks.

I shake my head.

'Hello?'

'Sorry,' I say. 'I haven't told her. Or anyone else.'

She nods. I hear it.

'Do you want me to?'

I sigh in relief. 'Yes. Yes. Thank you. Can you?'

'I don't know,' she replies.

How much can you really ask of people? Everything, I suppose. I can call in every favour now. Every single one.

'I would be so grateful if you would do it, please.'

I hear her crying again. But she has to take care of it, somehow she has to do it.

'I'm coming over,' she says, and we hang up.

Then I lie on my back. Close my eyes. A few weeks, six months, a few years. Right now I just need to close my eyes.

*

And they come. My friends all show up. I lie on the couch and look at them through half-closed eyes. They let me. They don't say much. They sit with their chins in their hands. Look at each other sometimes, and shake their heads. Shake them slowly, strangely. Like you do when the sorrow is bigger than it looks. When a sorrow stands for all sorrows. I know what they're thinking. We have lost so much. We have already lost so much. Why should we have to lose more. Why should it be like this, that we are forced to lose even more. I agree with them. They don't notice, they don't dare look at me, but I'm lying with my eyes half-closed shaking my head the same way. That strange way. When a sorrow stands for all sorrows.

Zahra and Leila and Anne and Firozeh. They're all here. They came right away, they were here within an hour. I didn't even manage to open my eyes before they were all here. I think of my notes, lying in the basket. The ones about my loneliness. I want to show them, say:

Why did you wait until now to come? Why didn't you come before, when I was so alone? But I don't know. At the same time, I feel I ought to tear those pages into a thousand pieces. Because I was never alone. Right? I don't know.

What is loneliness? Is it sitting alone wishing for company, or is it sitting alone waiting to die? Maybe I was never alone.

I hear them start to whisper. Don't listen at first, but soon I understand. They haven't told Aram. I want to stand up, make a scene. *I asked you for one thing! One single thing!* But I restrain myself. I know this is far from the first thing I've asked them for. Know it's asking too much.

Zahra rises, makes a call. Whispering. I can hear she's not talking to Aram, no. She's talking to someone else. She asks her own child to tell my daughter. What cowards we are! The revolutionaries. None of us has any guts. Maybe you only get a certain amount of guts in your life. Maybe we left ours on the bloody streets of revolution. I wonder who will tell Aram I'm dying. Realise I don't know, and that I won't get up to find out.

I often stand at the window looking out. My view is exquisite, like a painting. I point to it when I have a new visitor.

'Look,' I say. As if it were possible to avoid.

I live on the thirteenth floor, and one wall consists entirely of windows. Outside you see only sky. Sky, and sky never ending. Down below lies the sea, your eyes can follow it until it joins the horizon. And at the water's edge stands the forest. A thick line of trees that holds the seasons.

For most people it's nothing special. Sky, water, trees. I want to explain to them, to my visitors, exactly why it's so special. But I have a hard time making myself do so. I want to say to them: Do you know what I had around me when I was growing up? When I walked the streets, when I walked to school. Sand and stone. Sandy stone. It might be hard to visualise. Yellow sand that covered our shoes. That covered our houses. Our mother swept it out the door several times a day. Imagine, I who come from sand now live with sky and water. It's a transformation of elements. I want to say, this is immense. It's grand. It's also sad in a way. What you once were has disappeared. It has been replaced by something else.

But I say nothing, and I know why. I don't want them to

think I come from the desert. That I'm of a desert people. They already think that of me, and I refuse to plant more weird images of who I am in their heads. What I'm talking about is sand, not desert. They're two different things, but people wouldn't understand.

One thing about me, I just can't keep my mouth shut. I usually know when I should. At least in retrospect. But still I can't help blurting out what's on my mind. You're not supposed to do that. Not as a human. As a mother. You're supposed to keep your hurtful thoughts to yourself. But I can't.

I'm alone in my pain. I've come to that conclusion now. Aram should be the one to share this sorrow with me. Pain passes from woman to woman. But she doesn't.

She didn't come until four hours and forty-five minutes after I got the news. After I found out I was going to die. I know no one told her earlier. I know she didn't know. But I still feel annoyed. Yes, there are others here. But that's something else. They're sad. They will miss me. But my daughter ... She will never recover from this. We share that. I want to share that with her. The finality.

I'm still lying on the sofa with my eyes half-closed when she arrives. Everyone stands up and greets her. I hear her voice, it's tired. I want her to come in screaming. Screaming and weeping. In panic. But she doesn't. She enters and says hello to my friends and sounds tired. I don't get up. I let her come to me. She takes her time. Stands for a moment in the hall. She asks questions. Tries to understand. I know that is what she is doing. But it doesn't feel that way. It feels like she's standing around chatting, and it makes me angry. Here I am with everything falling apart, and it takes her four hours and forty-five minutes to show up, and even then she doesn't rush to me. She just stands there. I can feel my body tense up, my calves, buttocks, hands, face. When she does sit down on the rug next to me, I say nothing. I squeeze my eyelids shut.

'Hi, Mama,' she says.

'You have no mother,' I reply. 'You have nobody. You're an orphan.'

I hear her gasp, and everyone in the room along with her. I hear the pain I've created, the pain I sent into the air. I hear the grief. She's not the screaming and crying type, my daughter, I know that. So I hear how the grief plants itself in her body, making it hard for her to breathe. A little time passes, maybe a few minutes. Then she gets up and leaves. She goes into the bathroom to take care of herself. Just like she's always done.

I feel the tears well up and run down my face. Down into the folds in my neck. My friends cluster around me when they see me crying. Take my hand, stroke my head. Everyone surrounds me. She's over there, alone. I want to ask somebody to go to her, but the words won't come. She'll have to get used to it, says a voice in my head. If she's not already used to it, now's the time.

Aram reads poetry to me. She doesn't usually do that, and it surprises me. I think she used to do that kind of thing with Masood. Maybe she's hoping I can take her father's place. I can't. I sit on the sofa, and she sits down next to me with her legs folded beneath her.

'Mama, listen: *My father said: Since no one who belongs to you is buried in this earth this earth does not belong to you.*'

I stare emptily at her.

'Do you understand?' she asks me. '"Since no one who belongs to you is buried in this earth this earth does not belong to you." And now we've buried Dad.'

She watches my silence, filling it in, as if that would help.

'A Persian girl wrote that.'

I want to tell her it's ridiculous. First and foremost the earth belongs to no one, that's just patriotic crap. No one owns any land. *Your father was cremated*, I think. *The only thing inside the earth is his urn. He's not part of Swedish ground*. I'm the sort of person who says things like that. So I say it.

I hear myself say it out loud. I regret it instantly. I can see the pain shoot up from her chest, see her throat turn thick.

She's searching for meaning. Of course she is. She wants

to find a way to tie it all up, make a conclusion from all this chaos. I want to apologise, but I don't. I say:

'And if that's so, what happens after me? What happens when you've buried two of your parents here? Do they give you a medal? A Swedishness medal?'

She stands up and goes to the kitchen. Turns on the tap, pretending to get herself some water, I guess. I should go to her, but I don't. I lift up the remote and change the channel. It takes a minute or two for her to come back. She doesn't say much more. After a while she says:

'I'm going to go home now.'

I look at her in annoyance. 'You've only just got here.'

'I've been here for four hours, Mama. I have to go now.'

I don't want her to leave.

'If you're going to leave so soon, don't bother coming,' I hear myself say.

She nods. She leaves. I can't make her stay. It's been a long time since I managed to do that.

Is it possible you use up life faster if you live intensely? People have always told me I laugh too loud. Imagine if every laugh, every laugh that was too loud, took days off my life. What if you're only given a limited number of breaths, and they run out more quickly when you laugh too loud, talk too loud, dance yourself breathless. When you shout slogans and run from soldiers and guards. Breath, breath, pant, it all runs out. I wonder.

I've started treatment. It took three months. Easter got in the way.

'How much has the cancer spread in the last three months?'

I stare hard at the specialist, Christina. My eyes say, if I die, it's you, you and your waiting times, that are to blame.

Christina says nothing at first. She is trying to understand my question. She is both an oncologist and a gynaecologist. The cancer originated in my ovaries. It was my female parts, my mother parts, that caught fire. It was ironic. I told her so the first time we met, isn't it ironic how much we are punished for being women. That time too she looked at me like this. Silent. Wondering.

'It's hard to wait, I know,' she says. 'But we do our best.'

'You could have done your best three months ago! Then I might have had a chance.'

She looks down at her papers. 'We're admitting you now. For a few days.' That's all she says.

I hear Aram asking a lot of questions. Things I never would have thought to ask. She's done her research. I reach for her hand. She's the type who does her research.

'Are you a doctor?' Christina asks her.

'No,' she replies. 'No. This is my mother.' Her voice cracks, and I see the doctor hesitate.

In any case, I understand it's spread even further. They want to monitor me, in case the tumours cut off some bodily function. They talk about my bodily functions as if they're separate from me. I stop listening. Let Aram speak for me.

When they're finally done, we leave the small room. They have a bed ready for me, and I sit on the edge. Stare at the hospital gown, the greyish-white sheets. The blue blanket. Aram is still holding my hand.

'We'll make it like home, Mama.'

She leaves me to go and buy juice and newspapers, and I don't move. I don't move a millimetre while she's gone.

She comes back quickly, breathlessly. She has two bags in her hand, which she drops on the floor. She takes a few running steps and embraces me. Hard, hard, she holds me. I sit on the bed, my arms hanging at my sides, and I let them hang. I let her hold me. Resting in her arms. She hangs on to me for a long time. Rocking me gently. I feel her heart pounding against my cheek, and I think, I made that heart. Her heart once beat inside me, and now it beats against me, and soon it will beat without me. Soon, my heart will fall silent, and hers will beat on, carrying my rhythm with it. Somewhere in her heartbeat, I'll remain. I want the idea to be a comfort, but it's not. I want my own heartbeat. I want it for myself, and I want to carry it myself, and I don't want to exist as only a shadow in somebody else's body, in somebody else's memory.

I raise my hands and push her away, push her with force. She stumbles and almost falls backwards. She looks like a frightened child, like a lost baby bird thrown out of its nest with no warning. In my eyes, she meets nothing. I'm empty. She turns away in the end and fumbles for her bags. She sets the table. Bottles of juice. Magazines. All with pictures, intrusive paparazzi photos. She knows I don't have the energy to read. A bag of Werther's Originals, which she pours into a plastic cup. They remind me of my childhood, so far away in time and space. Then she picks up a small white rabbit with soft ears.

'I thought . . . I don't know if you want it.'

I take it in my arms. Caressing it while she fetches a vase and fills it with water from the tiny sink. She sets out flowers, one of those bouquets that will soon die. The kind you find in a hospital gift shop. I want to say, they're dying, just like me. But I hold back, try to hold back for just a little while. She sits down on the stool next to the bed.

'OK,' she says. 'OK. I have to go, I have to go to work.'

She holds my hand again. I let it lie limply in hers. 'When will you be back?'

'I'll come tomorrow, Mama. But I'll call tonight.'

Tomorrow. I look at the clock. 11.27 a.m. I count the hours I have to be in the hospital room alone, awake. I want to ask her to stay, but how do you do that. She says that she has to go, she doesn't want to stay. I feel a lump in my throat. No one wants to stay. I look up at her.

'Those ugly flowers will die soon,' I say. 'Just like me. You can take them with you.'

She jerks, as if I've slapped her in the face. Looks down at the floor. A few seconds pass, maybe a minute. It's quiet.

'Go then,' I say finally. And I turn away.

She rests her hand on my shoulder. Then she is gone.

My mother still doesn't know I'm dying. I haven't told her, and I've forbidden anyone else to do so either. Why should she have to be tormented by that thought? Why should she have to lose another daughter? Loss. Sometimes I want to say to those who accuse us of coming here to rip them off. To take something that isn't ours. I want to say to them, do you think I've won? Do you think I've gained more than I've lost? And you. Do you think you've lost more than I've gained? Do you think your loss is greater than my gain?

The day I was born, I was a disappointment. I was the sixth girl in a family with no sons. I was not what my parents had hoped for. But I wasn't the biggest disappointment. When Noora was born six years later, we were all deflated. I don't really know why they wanted boys. In more conservative families, a boy meant getting a breadwinner. A girl just cost money. But that wasn't the case with us. When I was born, Maryam was already twenty years old and a teacher. She moved out to the provinces, to the villages that needed teachers. She lived on her own and earned money. Money she brought home to us.

Soon all my older sisters worked. As teachers and research assistants. Their money was our money, and we lived in a cocoon of sisterhood and pride. My mother brought customers to our home. She cut and dyed their hair. She plucked their eyebrows and threaded their faces. I learned how early on, and I helped her. The women lay on a mattress, and I leaned over them with my back curved and a thread between my chubby baby fingers. I don't like to tell these things to people here in Sweden. It goes against the way they look at life here. My poor sisters who worked hard and had to give their money to their mother. Noora and I who swept up hair, threaded, and worked for the family. No real autonomy for them, no real childhood for us. One might say. But I think our lives were wonderful. My sisters, imagine the freedom they had. And me, with all these women, with the promise of femininity and self-sufficiency. All at the same time.

When I was young I had great potential. I was intelligent. Ambitious. Hard-working. Words you'd think might mean something. Lead to something.

I got into medical school. You can't imagine what an accomplishment that was. It was like a dream. The dream. My mother, my sisters. They were so proud they cried and cried for days after the notice of admission was published in the newspaper.

Towards the end of the summer my sisters invited our neighbours to a party, in celebration. My mother didn't like that. She didn't think you should advertise good news. The evil eye was what she feared the most. That some grudging person would look at us with envy, and their evil eye would destroy our world. But she helped us prepare anyway. We were eight women in a steamy kitchen. Mama and her seven daughters. It sounds like a fairy tale when you say it like that. I suppose it was.

Maryam, the sweat glistening on her forehead while she fried aubergine and cooked pot after pot of meat. Mahvash, Gita, Shoohreh and Shabnam in their miniskirts and bleached blonde blow-dries. Four independent, working women who looked like dolls. I was the one who cut and blow-dried their Farrah Fawcett hairstyles. That was the kind of world we pined for. *Charlie's Angels* and *The Godfather.* Strong and brittle. To save and be saved. Things that don't really exist in any reality. They sat on the floor with their legs stretched out and cleaned vegetables and Mama glared at those long, bare legs and eventually she hid them with a blanket. She didn't want us to show any skin. Show off. She didn't want us to provoke.

And then Noora. Our baby, just turned twelve. She ran between us with her braids bouncing in the air and talked. Boy, how she prattled on.

'I don't understand why we can't invite *agha* Hossein and his boys?'

'We can't, Noora,' our mother replied.

'But I don't understand why. We've known them all our lives. Won't they be offended?'

'They don't want to come, Noora.'

'But how do we know, did we ask?'

Maryam stepped in in those situations, when she sensed our mother's energy was flagging. That was always her role. Deflect, protect, take over.

'Noora, they don't want to come because they're ashamed to come.'

'But why are they ashamed?'

'Because Mustafa was here and asked for Nahid's hand and she said no, remember? That kind of thing isn't easy for a man, Noora.'

'But that only shows that he likes her, so it's obvious he wants to be here and celebrate.'

'No, Noora. It's not obvious.'

Me, I was the opposite of Maryam. Short and hard, no interest in protecting anyone.

'It's just the reverse. He's a man and his pride is all he has. Do you think he can handle the girl who said no to him making something of herself? Becoming a doctor? When no one in his family, not one of six healthy boys and men, has gone to university? Half of them didn't even finish high school. They don't want to celebrate us! They're probably sitting around calling us witches and whores.'

'Nahid!'

I lowered my head and fell silent. Maryam rarely spoke sharply.

'Witches and whores!' Noora laughed delightedly and danced across the kitchen floor. 'Witches and whores,' she sang, and Mahvash and Gita sang along.

Noora lifted the blanket Mama had placed over them. With a coquettish wink she threw it over her head like a *chador.*

'Witches and whores they said of Dr Nahid, witches and whores, that's what we are.'

I met Maryam's eyes and we both started laughing. Soon we were all on our feet, someone had put on a vinyl record, and we sang and danced with lettuce and meat cleavers in our hands. Witches and whores gave way to Hayedeh, a pop icon.

I remember years later. Long after we fled. Long after Hayedeh fled. When the news of her death reached us, Masood barely looked up from his newspaper. Just said three words:

'One less whore.'

When I remember that party, the feeling of loss cuts even deeper. It was so perfect. My sisters and mother cooked for days. Our uncle hung lanterns across the yard. He invited some musician friends, too. A singer with a silky voice, an elderly man on a tombak and his son on sitar. Neighbours and relatives flowed through the garden gate. They whistled and cheered, excited about the future. Even *agha* Hossein came by. He stopped at the door and held his hat to his chest and waited. After I cautiously approached him he cleared his throat.

'Congratulations,' he said, handing over a small gift.

I rushed to kiss him on the cheek. It was as if his presence confirmed my every hope for the life that awaited me. Everything would turn out fine, and nothing was as bad as I feared. He turned and left without saying any more, but it didn't matter. I followed his back with my eyes until he disappeared through his own door, and then I ran over to my sisters again. Ran like a child.

The musicians sang and played everything we asked them to, and we took turns running to them with expectant eyes and a request for the next song. We danced. I don't even think any of us ate any of the food. We danced and we sang. There were no nuances. No shadows. Only joy. My mother was sending a daughter to medical school. The sole provider to seven girls. She stayed away, but finally Noora ran into the kitchen and pulled her out. We grabbed her by the arms and pushed her and she laughed and stepped into our ring and threw the tea towel over her shoulder and danced. She danced and sang, and when the song was over, she came up to me and took my face between her rough hands, angular and calloused from all those years in the salon. She kissed my forehead. Long and hard. Noora whistled, and I closed my eyes to hide the tears welling up. Then she left and stayed inside for the rest of the evening, but it didn't matter. I knew I'd given her something meaningful.

He was there that night. We had never met him before. The Soltani family brought him along. He'd just moved to the city to study at the university. They thought it was fitting. Thought he'd like meeting other students. I didn't notice him at first, what I noticed was that Noora was talking to someone for a long time. Someone who was laughing at her jokes and listening to her bubbling thoughts and observations. It was only later in the evening, when I sat on the steps with my platform shoes next to me, rubbing my sore feet, that she pulled him over. That I saw him.

'Nahid. Nahid, this is Masood! He's going to be studying agriculture. His father is a farmer! What is it he raises? Oh yeah, worms! Silkworms! And they spin threads and the threads make carpets and ... It's very important work! The pride of Iran. Can you imagine!'

Masood laughed. A warm, chuckling laugh. Not self-conscious, or formed in the mouth, but a real laugh, the kind that comes from deep in the belly.

'For my father, it's very important, but the pride of Iran it is not. I don't know if we have any pride left.'

Those words made me look up. When I met his eyes they were both inviting and defiant.

'I thought *we* were the pride of Iran. Its beautiful women.'

I said the words as if it were natural for me to say such things. To flirt. It was not. I'd never done it before. I remember hoping Noora wouldn't make fun of me, hoping she'd let me get away with it.

He sat down on the steps next to me. Smiled so all his teeth were exposed.

'You're not our pride, you're our heart.'

Noora whistled. 'Don Juan. Warning: Don Juan!'

Then she ran away and we stayed sitting there. I had no idea I had so much to talk about. Had so much going on in my head. But he seemed to know, know exactly.

We talked, Masood and me. We talked as the music fell silent and the lamps went out. We talked as friends and neighbours came up and kissed my cheeks, congratulating me one last time. We sat on the steps and talked all that first night. Maryam peered out between the curtains from time to time, watching over us.

He had ideas, more radical than any I'd ever heard. Ideas about tearing down all the old structures that locked us into our destinies. He talked about the people, about the people's right to bread. He spoke of justice as if it were a party, as if it were our job to arrange it. Send out the invitations. As the sun rose, he leaned back and rested on his arms, eyes closed. His fair hair curled at his forehead and gleamed like gold in the morning light. I looked at him, not the least bit tired. I remember that feeling so well. The feeling of having been awake all night, of having danced until my feet ached, having sung and talked until my throat was crackling dry, but still not being satisfied. On the contrary, I wanted more. That hunger.

I think that's what life is. Being hungry. I'm trying to think of anything now that would be worth staying awake all night for. Nothing comes to me, not a solitary thought. Am I full now, I wonder. Maybe that is why the cancer came to me.

Masood came back a few evenings later. I sat on the kitchen floor, in Papa's old place, hemming my skirts on Mama's sewing machine. Beside me the radio blared, and I swayed to the music. The feeling from the party was still with me, pristine. There weren't many days left until the university term started, and I had so much faith in that place. In what could happen when thinking people were brought together. In my naivety the length of my skirt was a primary concern, was one of my first thoughts. I should have shorter skirts. I should be a free woman with free legs.

Suddenly Noora came running in and threw herself on the floor next to me. Her eyes sparkled behind thick glasses, and in her hand she held a large bouquet of flowers.

'He's here, he's back! He's here to see you, Nahid!'

I waved at her to turn down the volume on the radio. 'Who, Noora, who's here?'

'Who? What do you mean who? As if you aren't thinking about him all the time. Masood of course, he's back. He's in love with you, Nahid, I'm sure of it. Oh, can you believe it? Someone's in love with you! A doctor and loved. How does it feel, Nahid?'

I pulled her to me, laughing. Kissed her forehead.

'I love you, kiddo, you know that? You're the one who's loved.'

She tore loose. Always in such a hurry.

'He's waiting for you, Nahid. He's standing outside waiting, he didn't want to come in and disturb us. But the flowers are for me! They're not yours. I got them because I set you up.'

She buried her face in the bouquet and breathed in deeply.

'They smell like love!'

I stood up and went to him.

I arrived on registration day wearing my short-short skirt, with my hair blow-dried into soft waves that curled on my shoulders. The blouse I wore was Gita's, a soft silk with a bow on the chest. I have a photo somewhere. Of me and my mother next to each other at the gate just before I go. She's a head shorter with a broad smile on her face. Her smiles were rare. I have a childish, playful expression. Noora must have been standing behind the camera.

I know I felt proud on that day, at that moment. Proud and happy. I should have been satisfied with what I had. Not grasped for more. But I did anyway.

The cliques were clear from the first day. People stood in clusters, many spoke quietly, but there were also those who already had slogans. You heard them, like the first popcorn kernels to pop in the pot. One here, one there. Not all the time, not often, but clearly. With a promise that there would be more. I walked with my folders pressed to my chest and my wooden heels clacking on the mosaic beneath my feet. It didn't feel so right any more. It didn't feel so free. The girls in those clusters dressed like boys. They wore bellbottoms and button-up shirts with their faces bare of makeup and their hair in braids. They moved freely, effortlessly. They were illuminated. As if they wanted something so big that the largeness of the idea itself lit them up.

I was supposed to meet Masood at the cafeteria, and I saw him before he saw me. He was leaning against the wall with a cigarette in his mouth, gesturing energetically. He was surrounded by people. One of those groups. I froze, suddenly overcome with intense shame. Ashamed of my bare legs and all the energy I'd put into dressing up for freedom. What did I know about being free? I almost turned around to go, but he saw me. Our eyes met, and he stopped mid-sentence. I don't know how to explain that kind of thing. Thinking about it now, I despise my own naivety. But in that moment. He lit up when he saw me. As if with life itself. His face shone with joy and admiration, and the longer he looked at me the more my insecurity fell away. It didn't matter what clothes I was wearing or what doubts I had. I felt that he saw who I was. That he saw what I wanted. That he'd help me get it. I felt that he wanted my freedom and strength, might even want it more than I did.

It was a warm evening a few weeks later. I'd sat in the library with my books until late. I used to rush home after lectures to help my mother, but something was happening to me at the university. I think I started to feel like I was a person in and of myself. That I existed beyond my relationship to others. It was a completely new idea, and it lasted about as long as a fart.

I didn't take the bus home, instead I strolled through the city. Looking at young people in love. A couple whispering to each other on a park bench. Another couple arguing loudly in front of an ice cream stall. It wasn't for me, had never been for me. I didn't want to be somebody's wife. I didn't want to devote my life to caring for others. I didn't want to turn out like my mother. The last thing I wanted was to turn out like my mother. But I couldn't stop thinking about love. About Masood. I wanted to be with him, but not belong to him. And it doesn't work that way, it never has.

When I finally opened the gate, the lights were off. I thought they were sleeping, my mother and Noora. But as I crossed the small courtyard and opened the front door, I heard singing in the kitchen. Must be the radio, I thought as I hung up my jacket and unpacked my books in the hall. But the voice reminded me of someone, and I heard something else. Running water. I tiptoed to the kitchen, and the first thing I saw was my mother. She was sitting in her usual seat with her eyes closed and a teacup cradled in her hands. She rocked gently back and forth, rocking herself along with the song. I stepped in and was startled to see Masood's back. He stood at the sink with his sleeves rolled up, doing the dishes with tender movements while he sang.

They hadn't noticed that I'd come in, and I didn't want to disturb their tranquillity so I left them. I left them and went to my bed, looked at Noora who was sound asleep in the bed next to mine, listened to the soft singing coming from the kitchen, and I remember that my eyes filled with tears. His presence gave me a sense of security I'd never felt before.

One Friday morning at dawn Masood knocked lightly on our door. I ran towards him. I'd stashed the skirts and blouses in the back of my closet. Instead, I wore bellbottoms, comfortable shoes, and one of Noora's plaid school shirts. My face was free of makeup, and I bristled a little as he embraced me. I felt bare and exposed, more naked than I ever felt in short skirts. But that would change. Soon, I wouldn't see myself as a face any more, but as a bundle of thoughts and ideas. And they protected me more than makeup ever had.

We were headed up into the mountains for a meeting with the others. The people Masood was standing with on registration day had become our group. We needed to avoid police and soldiers, and the proud mountains swallowed us whole.

We drove Masood's car out of the city, but parked it a safe distance from the foot of the mountains. Then we hiked up. Building strength, building stamina. Resistance. It was magical. The sun burned low on the horizon. The air was clear and still a bit chilly. The adrenaline pumped through our bodies. Feet steadily tramping on, steadily carrying us forward. That special sound of feet. Feet that trek, feet that run, feet that struggle.

As we approached the meeting place, Masood started forming sounds in his mouth. A tone that meant we were there. Another that meant no one was following us. And then came the answer. The sound that meant the coast was clear.

They were expecting us. Saber and Rozbeh and Ali and Soraya. That was before we had assumed names, before we started living underground in hiding. Back then it was something other than what it became. We greeted each other with warm kisses on the cheek and excited voices. Ali served tea and Saber, our leader, started the meeting. He was leaning forward with one foot on a rock, his arms resting on his thigh. The sight set off butterflies in my stomach. Saber's shirtsleeves were rolled up, and he wore a thin vest and heavy shoes. A cascade of mountain peaks at his back. They shone yellow in the sunlight, and they looked so powerful. I think we saw ourselves as part of those mountains. We thought we were just as powerful. Just as steady. Immortal. A people of stone.

When we were finished with politics, Rozbeh lifted his sitar and started to play. From where we sat we could see other groups, hundreds of people. Music came from many directions. Harmonica, song. Masood whistled along, and Soraya sang. *Now winter is over, and spring is in bloom.* After the first verse, I joined in. *The red flower of the sun is back, and the night is over.* We sat there with our boots and berets and braids and bare faces. *In our breasts are forests of stars.*

That's how it started for us.

The revolution fell upon us like a rain of stars. I'm not sure when we realised it was a revolution we were part of. That we were revolutionaries. We wanted to be, of course. But it began like a childish dream. Children dreaming of being astronauts, or movie stars, or president.

When we met Saber he was about to graduate as an engineer. He was like a lion. So handsome. So big. So strong. You could see the strength rippling through the muscles on his back as he walked in front of us. Everyone was in love with him, boys and girls. You don't meet very many people like that in your life. I suppose I'm glad I had the opportunity. Still, I wish I'd never seen him. Never met Masood. Wish he'd never come to our house. Wish I'd wandered around campus in my miniskirts and lived life as it was.

I think now, we were idiots. We had everything. We had everything you could really wish for. We were the most fortunate people in our country. In many ways, we had more than the truly rich. We had a future to build with our own hands. Saber. He should have been satisfied with becoming a well-dressed man with a beautiful wife and a house and kids and cars and whisky. But no. We constructed principles. We wanted true freedom. We wanted it for ourselves, but above all we wanted it for everyone else. That was the attraction, the beauty. To bear the weight of justice on our shoulders. To be soldiers for justice.

We thought it was in our hands! That it was something we could enact. Naive, idiotic children. But it was the best thing I've done in my life. Sometimes I wish it had been my life. What came later . . . That I could have done without.

Noora and I crept out of bed long before sunrise that day. We dressed in thrilling anticipation. Mama didn't hear us. I remember for a moment thinking we should wake her. I should tell her that Noora was coming with us this time. But I didn't. I was afraid she would protest and that Noora would be disappointed. I let Mama sleep, and Noora and I went to meet Masood who was waiting for us in the courtyard.

When I look back on it, I know this was a few years later, but it all feels like a single movement. The transfer of power had taken place, and we weren't satisfied. The universities had been closed to silence people like us. But we continued. With our meetings, with our demonstrations.

I don't know why we let her come along. I still can't understand why. She wanted to so badly. She'd been nagging us for so long. She was so excited by our words. By what she saw between us. By our comrades who came and went, the whispers and loud laughter.

'The struggle is as much mine as yours,' she said to me, and Masood laughed. We couldn't disagree with her. Our sweet little Noora. A fourteen-year-old woman warrior.

We took her hands and set out into the darkness. We met up with the rest of the group under the bridge. Saber nodded at Noora. A silent gesture that made her grow several centimetres. Then he motioned for us to follow him, and we did. At a gate we didn't recognise, he stopped and waved for Masood and me to come inside. The others stayed outside and kept watch. We went down into a dark basement. It took a few seconds for my eyes to adjust, and I remember my hand searching for Masood's. We held each other tight. A woman stood up from her place in front of a hot printing press and walked over to us. She handed Saber a stuffed canvas bag, without saying a word.

Out on the street, we divided the newly printed leaflets between us, and Saber pointed out each person's route. We thought we were seasoned by then. We'd done it so many times by now. Going around the city pushing our flyers under doors. We spread our message. Encouraging and stirring up the masses. The flyers all said basically the same thing, though we put so much time and energy into the wording.

Resistance.

Struggle.

Justice.

Equality.

Freedom.

Saber had given Noora her own stack, but I didn't dare let her go alone.

'Give me those!' she protested. 'Nahid! I want to, Nahid. These are mine.'

'You can go with me. That's good enough.'

I snatched the leaflets from her hand and our eyes met. She looked at me as if I'd stolen something from her. An experience. Like a night at the movies or a new pair of shoes.

'Noora, this is serious! You come with me.'

Noora stretched to take back the flyers, but Masood stood in the way. He put his hands on her shoulders. Looked at her with the paternal gaze I knew she needed.

'We love you too much, Noora,' he said.

She let her arms drop. Gave in.

Masood smiled at me, and Noora and I walked away. To be caught with those leaflets in your hands would mean execution. We knew that, and it didn't stop us. But Noora. We couldn't put that on her.

Noora walked a few steps behind me all morning, and it uplifted me. To have her there. I was proud of her courage. Sometimes she forgot herself. Started skipping, or humming a song, and then I couldn't stop myself from laughing. But mostly, we crept. Crouched and swore when we saw someone approaching. Hid in narrow alleys. Her eyes glittered. She liked it, and I understood her. It was fun. It was thrilling. It was scary, but like a haunted house is scary. And we had each other.

When we'd delivered our stack, we met up with Masood and Rozbeh. The sun started to rise over the rooftops, and we walked together down the street. Down the middle of the street we went. As if nothing could touch us. As if we were immortal. The sun crept over us. Watching us.

'This is freedom,' said Noora. She said it solemnly, and I felt life itself tingling inside me. Masood took off his beret and pushed it down onto her head. He laughed. Put his arm around her and pressed her to him.

She was fourteen, I was twenty. I wonder what sisters do together at that age. What they talk about. My mind is blank, I don't know. I know what I did with my sister, and I know that it was wonderful. It was like a dream. It lives inside me like a dream.

We walked together towards the university, where there was supposed to be a demonstration. When Noora realised we were actually letting her come along, she ran over to me from behind and jumped on my back.

'*Zendegi, jonami jan!*' Life!

We laughed together. She and I, and the others, at her childish eagerness.

When I think back, I wonder why nobody was worried. Why no one was afraid. Why no one ran the other way. Went home. Hid.

In front of the university a thousand, maybe several thousand people were gathered. We flowed into the crowd and were dragged along, Masood, Rozbeh, Noora and me. We held hands, moved as a chain. It was important. Important to dissolve the group and spread out so that not everyone was exposed to the same danger at the same time. And important that we stayed together. We held hands, and we yelled out slogans. The sun beat down on us, and I glanced at Noora a few times. Wondered if the crowd scared her. Wondered if she could stand it, if she would ask to go home. She didn't. She shouted as if the struggle was hers, hers personally. Fourteen years old.

It is difficult to distinguish one moment from the next.

The movement was somehow like a trance. I don't know how long we were out there. But suddenly the march stopped, and we heard screams ahead of us. Screams and bangs. Masood tried to climb up on Rozbeh's shoulders to see what was happening, but just then the crowd turned. People started running in panic towards us, gone were those excited faces. Masood and Rozbeh fell, and I pulled Noora after me in their direction. I don't know how we managed to find them and get them back on their feet, but we did. Then we ran, our hands still linked. Masood tried to find a way out, but it was too crowded. We could only go with the flow. Then there was a bang right in front of us, and for a moment everything froze. That moment when we all realised that the guards were driving into the crowd with their motorcycles and weapons. They were everywhere.

There was no longer any direction, any unity. The human sea moved like a whirlwind. Everyone was looking for a gap, a way out. It took a while until I understood. The finality of how bad it had got. How much worse it would get. But then I met Masood's gaze and it was full of a terror I'd never even imagined. They were shooting to kill. I turned to Noora. She looked at me behind her big round glasses, smiling, puzzled. She thought this was how it was supposed to be. She wondered what we were going to do now. What the next step would be. I smiled at her. Nodded, to keep her calm.

Everything happened in one motion. I know we were never still. But that moment is so vivid, so deeply etched onto my retinas, my head, my heart, that it is as though everything stood still. As though we stood on a stage with spotlights directed at us, at the very centre of the universe. I nodded towards Noora. Heard a shot that made me jump. It sounded close. More than that. It felt like something passed by, close to me. I turned to Masood again. So fast that my braids whipped me in the face. Then I felt a heaviness, an incongruous weight in my hand. I looked down. It was Rozbeh. He fell. Hit his knees on the ground. He looked up at me, face contorted. His grip on my hand slackened, and he slid down onto his stomach. It didn't hit me at first. It didn't hit me that something had afflicted us. The crowd was so large. We were so young. Why would anything happen to us? I bent to grab his hand again. Get him on his feet. But then Masood also fell down on his knees. He fell down hard and grabbed Rozbeh's torso, pulling it against himself. And I saw it. The blood blooming like a flower on the white of Rozbeh's T-shirt. The red rose on his chest. Masood turned his head to the sky. His eyes were closed, and he roared. I think I just stood there and stared. Then I pulled off my scarf. Pressed it to the wound. But the blood continued to flow. It spread in an ever-widening circle. I screamed for help, but there was no help to be had. And then he disappeared. One moment he was looking into my eyes with a pained expression, and the next he was gone.

'We'll take him with us,' said Masood. 'Lift him! Rozbeh, *dadash*, we've got you. We've got you, Rozbeh.'

Masood tried to lift him, get him onto his back. But the crowd pushed in, and he couldn't maintain his balance. He fell with the body on top of him, and they lay there amid all those running feet.

'He's dead. Masood, Masood. Do you hear me? He's dead.'

He shook his head. Continued pressing on the bullet hole. Kept talking, kept trying to calm the lifeless body.

Finally he held him in his arms. Sat there, in the middle of everything, holding Rozbeh, screaming his name.

Only then did I realise that Noora was no longer with us. I had let go of her hand. The crowd pressed in around us, and the smoke lay thick above our heads. Noora was gone. I too began to scream.

We screamed those names. Rozbeh. Noora. Names who were people to us, our people. Our voices couldn't be heard, but we stood there and howled those names, and people ran by and trampled on us, and the shots exploded through our cries.

It was a minute. It was no more than a minute. It feels like for ever. It feels like my whole life.

*

It took a while for Masood to hear me. Before he understood that we'd lost her. But then he looked at me and jumped up from the ground. We left Rozbeh, we left him there between the bodies and rifle shots. We didn't know which way to go, where she could have gone. In the end we just started running. We ran together and cried out her name. We ran and ran, and I thought he was right behind me. I thought I heard his cries. I thought I felt his body close to mine. So I turned into an alley and thought he'd turn too, and steps followed me so I assumed they were his. Thought we'd found cover. We could talk about what to do now. How to find Noora. But when I turned around someone else was there. A man dressed in black with a cudgel in his hand. We stood there face to face. He was no older than me. We were two children staring at each other. And then I realised that he was one of them, he was one of the ones who had killed Rozbeh. My thoughts bounced like ping-pong balls in my head. Should I kick, run, climb, do anything I could to get away? Or should I smile and play innocent. Say I was on my way home, I just happened to end up in the middle of this wretchedness, my mother would be worried if I didn't get home soon. But a grin spread across his face, and it scared me. I realised we were alone in an alley, and he could do whatever he wanted to me. Nobody could protect me from him. I think that thought took over. A fear of death, in a way. Being raped by him would be worse than dying. I have to get past him, was my only thought. I have to get past him and into the street. I didn't want to get stuck there, out of sight, violated, humiliated. So I clenched my fists and bent my knees. Felt a scream rising from my gut and I went for him. Like when a character in a Bruce Lee movie runs up and over their opponent. I don't know how it happened, but suddenly I was out on the street and back inside the crowd again. I tried to push myself forward, zigzag, but it was smoky and hard to see, and there were too many people. I was suddenly so tired. He caught up. Grabbed me from behind. I screamed! I screamed for Noora, and I screamed for Masood.

'I have to find my sister. Please, please. She's a child.'

He raised his arm and backhanded my face. The physical pain. I wasn't prepared for it. I remember that so clearly, how it surprised me. Not even the shot that split Rozbeh's chest had prepared me for it. The fight fizzled out of my body, and I fell silent. It was clear that they were going to arrest me. They could arrest me and torture me and kill me if they wanted to. As long as I wasn't raped, I just didn't want to be raped. I would have rather died, I'd rather have died than be forced to give myself to them. It would have been like being injected with evil, to go around the rest of my life carrying it. Living with evil rippling inside me.

*

He dragged me across the ground. The gravel cut into my back, and I closed my eyes. I didn't want to see. I didn't want to guess. I'd have gone voluntarily if he'd given me the chance. But he liked it. Forcing me. Then he grabbed me around the waist and threw me into the back of a waiting truck. It was pitch dark inside. Bodies everywhere. Moaning, screaming. I kept my eyes closed. I kept my eyes closed until the doors opened again, and they started pulling us out. Behind me, a guy shouted in a shrill voice:

'They're going to shoot us! Comrades, let us sing, let us join our voices in song!'

I turned to hush him, but he just smiled at me. He smiled like everything was fine. The men in black pushed me aside and grabbed him. The rest of us just stared. We said nothing. We didn't sing along. We just stared. They dragged him over the ground, away towards a wall. An elderly woman took my arm, dug her nails deep into my skin. I closed my eyes again. We heard him. We all heard his song. Then a shot rang out through the air and everything fell silent. It was the harshest silence I've heard in my life.

*

They detained so many people that day. When you think about it, really allow yourself to think about it, it's surreal. So many bodies. I was reminded of it when Göran Persson talked about a meat mountain, wondered if he'd ever seen a real meat mountain, a mountain of human bodies. It wasn't that we were lying on each other or that we were dead. Not in my cell anyway, though I know that a mountain of dead flesh was nearby. But there were so many of us, in such a small area, with so many bodily fluids rubbed between us. Blood, sweat, tears, urine. I pushed my way in, through it all. My eyes searched for Noora. *Please let us be in the same place*, I thought. *Let me take care of her. I need to take care of her.* But I didn't see her. *She's not here. Of course she's not here. She's home with Mama. She has to be.*

I slumped down in a corner. It felt safer that way. Being tightly enclosed by two walls and out of sight. I sat there a very long time. Slowly the room emptied, one body after another. I followed each person with my eyes. They disappeared, and no one came back. I tried not to think about where they went.

I was one of the last to be led out. Two men in black clothes grabbed me by the arms. They smelled bad. Sour sweat. I who always yelled and argued, I was silent. In silence I stared at their hands. Their hands. They were big, calloused. Covered with bruises and small cuts. They were hands that had given thousands of lashes. Hands that burned cigarettes against thin skin, that wrapped themselves around panting throats.

They took me into an interrogation room and left me there. It was dark except for the light from an oil lamp that stood on a rickety metal table. Behind the table was a folding chair. I didn't know what to do. If I was supposed to sit down. So I backed away instead, pressed myself against the wall with my arms wrapped around my body. My entire body was shaking, and I wished I had cyanide tablets. Masood and I had discussed it, that we would rather swallow cyanide and die than be tortured and murdered by them. But I don't think we believed it would actually happen, not so soon. I thought it sounded brave. Take your own life, refuse to let it be taken by others. I thought it was something a real warrior would do. But I realised in the interrogation room that the opposite was true. It was my fear that made me wish I could kill myself.

A thin man in a grey suit entered. He had a sparse beard that he seemed to be growing out. He wore a drab yellow polo shirt under his jacket. He came in alone, cradling a stack of papers, but when he saw me he shouted into the hallway, and two more men in black arrived to escort him to the small table. Then he sat down, and they stood behind him.

He began by asking a series of yes or no questions. Was I a Muslim? Did I pray regularly? Was I a Marxist? Did I support the Islamic Revolution?

That is not my revolution! I screamed inside. But on the outside, I nodded to every question on Islam and shook my head at every mention of communism or the red struggle. I didn't hesitate. During our meetings we'd talked about this very situation. Should we stand up for our ideals even when our lives were at stake. It seemed obvious then that we should. Anything else would be a betrayal. An opportunistic betrayal. But I didn't. I was too scared to stand up for what I thought I was fighting for. I wanted to live. I didn't want to die.

But then they wanted information.

'Who told you to go out on the street?' asked the thin man. He slammed his pen to the paper. Every word I said he wrote down.

'No one,' I replied. And it was true. I was the one who'd told people to go out. I was one of those they wanted to remove, eliminate.

They asked whom I had been with, and I hesitated. It would help if I said something. I wouldn't suffer as much if I gave them something. So I said Rozbeh's name. I figured they couldn't arrest him. They couldn't take his life again.

I told them this was my first time. That I didn't really know what the demonstration was about. That Rozbeh was my fiancé. He'd said we'd just stop by quickly, and afterwards we'd go to the movies. I was just following him. I blamed everything on him and mentioned no other names. I said I didn't care about politics. I just followed my fiancé.

'Will you do it again?' the man asked.

'No. Never.'

He looked down at his papers again. Wrote down the words precisely.

'*Agha*, I just want to get married and have children and live my life. Please. What happened today has nothing to do with me.'

He hummed and wrote. I didn't dare look up at the black-clad men. I just looked at him. I wondered which laws he was following. Which laws he would consult when deciding what to do with me.

In the end, he pushed a stack of papers across the table. 'Sign here.'

I glanced at him to try to deduce what he meant, and then leaned over the papers and started to read.

'Sign it!'

Now it was one of the black-clad men who shouted, and I scrambled for the pen. I caught a glimpse of the last few lines before I signed my name. It said that I swore my allegiance to the Islamic revolution.

The black-clad men grabbed me under the arms again and threw me out a door. It was not the door I'd entered through. I felt my heart skip a beat. They didn't believe me, I thought. They'd sent me out through the other door. I stood up and staggered through the corridor. There were no doors and no windows. Not a single person. But I heard screaming. I heard blows. For a moment I stood still and listened. Listening for Noora. But the sounds were indistinguishable from each other. I walked down the corridor and around a corner and came upon another door. A larger door.

I stared at it for a long time. We'd heard so many stories, why hadn't I realised this was real? That it could happen to me? I sank down on the floor. Threw my arms around my knees. Tried to calm my breathing. A clear image of what stood on the other side of the door floated into my mind. A courtyard. Rows of people. Blindfolds. Black-clad men with guns. Bodies falling to the ground. Bodies being dragged away. New people in rows. I'd heard every detail. But some people ended up there and still got away. Those stories would never have reached me if it weren't possible to escape. *I can escape!* That's what I thought. *I'm one of the ones who can escape*. So I got up again. Went over to the door and opened it. Gently. I tried to look out, see something, prepare myself.

It was pitch dark and cold, and I knew it was night. I heard nothing, so I stepped out. The door slammed shut behind me. Only darkness and silence remained. I was alone. My first impulse was to turn around and try to open the door again, but it was locked. So I ran. I ran straight out, straight ahead, without any idea where I was or where I was going. And no one stopped me. They'd let me go.

I walked for a long time across an open field before I came to a road. I kept looking over my shoulder the whole way. Thinking, there must be some mistake. They were surely going to come after me. But no one came.

At dawn a truck drove by, and I raised my arms, signalling for help. I wasn't sure it was the right thing to do, but I was afraid I wouldn't make it out there. I'd thought I was capable of escaping a firing squad, but I wasn't even capable of withstanding cold and desolation.

The truck dropped me off in the middle of the city. At the very same square where I'd been separated from Masood, Noora and Rozbeh. I couldn't say if that had happened yesterday or several days ago.

I wanted the square to look just like it had before everything happened. I wanted it to be standing there, stately, with the statue of the Shah in the middle of the roundabout and John Wayne posters hanging on the cinema walls. I wanted to turn back the revolution to the last dictatorship, the old shit. Or at least I wanted to turn back time to any point where I could have chosen to stay out of it.

It was only after I jumped out of the truck that I remembered they'd taken my handbag. I didn't have a cent on me. So I started walking again. I walked and walked. It was an endless walk. I kept thinking as I walked, it's not easy to fight. The fight is not easy. It's not easy to fight. It played in a loop in my head. It's not easy to fight.

*

I mumbled to myself all the way home. 'Noora's already home,' I said. 'She's a smart girl. Young. Fast. She ran away. Ran home to Mama.'

I nodded.

'They're sitting in the kitchen right now. Drinking tea

and Mama is saying, "Nahid better get home soon." Noora laughs. Noora laughs and says "Of course she's coming home, Mama." That's how it is. Masood is out buying bread for them. They'll all three look at me when I walk through the door. They'll yell at me and laugh at me and hug me. And then it will all be over, everything will be over, no big deal. No big deal.'

When I turned the corner to our street, it was my mother I first saw. She was sitting on a stool outside the gate. She was rocking back and forth with her hands on her thighs. I could see someone had placed a tray of tea at her feet. She hadn't touched the glass. I felt so ashamed when I saw her that I wanted to turn back.

As I approached, I saw my mother's eyes were closed and her lips moving. She was reciting a poem by Hafiz. She whispered it, whispered as one whispers a prayer. I put my hand on her shoulder, and she opened her eyes and looked at me like a ghost had stepped through her dreams. She stared at me for several seconds before she threw herself from the footstool. She threw herself with such force that the stool crashed onto the tea tray and the dishes broke into a thousand pieces. But she didn't notice. She threw herself onto the ground at my feet and flung her arms around my legs. She shouted my name in a voice as shattered as the glass on the ground. I fell down beside her, and we held each other. She screamed, and I listened. I wished I too could scream, but it was as if the part of me capable of that was frozen solid.

'*Maman. Maman*,' I said finally. 'Where is Noora?'

That moment. If I could somehow erase that moment from my life, from my memory, from my retinas. My mother's uncomprehending stare. She assumed I was the one who knew where Noora was. She assumed Noora was safe. The confusion that transformed to terror, pure terror, and then her body falling to the ground next to me, where she curled up into a ball and screamed. Screamed a new name, her baby's name. I wanted to lie down next to her, press myself against her and draw comfort from her round motherly body, but I feared she might die there. Feared her heart might burst and stop. She gasped for breath, and I thought: I have killed her. So I ran inside and called an ambulance. They lifted her up onto a stretcher and Mahvash and Gita rode along. My sisters didn't look at me. They refused to look at me.

After they left, I walked through the house. Looked in every room. Finally I went into the room we shared, Noora and I. Her bed was carefully made up. The pyjamas she wore lay folded on the bedspread. I lifted them and walked out again. Sat down on my mother's stool and breathed in the scent of the soft fabric. Cats. I remember that. There were cats on her pyjamas.

Masood came towards me in the dark. Finally, he came. His clothes were torn, and he was dirty. Sand and mud everywhere. He came on foot, like me. I wondered if he'd been in the same interrogation room, answered the same way I had. If they had released him and he had breathed in the cool night air and started walking. But I knew better. He would never say what they wanted to hear. He would never nod to Islam and shake his head at Marxism. He would never name names.

He was the type they'd take out through one of the other doors. They'd never let him escape, into the darkness. A darkness reserved for traitors.

I was sitting on the stool when he came. Sitting completely still and staring straight ahead. It was like I'd been holding my breath and could finally inhale. I breathed in deeply and then I screamed, straight out. He ran towards me and put his head in my lap. We cried together, I think it was the only time we cried together. We should have done it often, many more times. If only we'd cried together instead of letting the pain turn into a thorn between us, maybe our lives wouldn't have turned out like this. Maybe then we wouldn't have been so alone. Maybe then he wouldn't be dead. And I wouldn't be dying.

'I went to Rozbeh's house,' he said. 'I wanted to tell his parents. But the gate was broken, and I saw guards in the courtyard. I don't understand. How did they identify him? Why are they going after his parents? They're arresting innocent people, people who've just lost a son.'

I froze where I sat. I sat completely still. And I decided to never tell anyone. Not about the interrogation room or the questions. Not that I'd reported Rozbeh, given them his name. His poor parents. My mother. These tormented souls.

'Noora is gone,' I said to Masood.

Something happened in his eyes when he heard my words. His loving, despairing brown eyes. It was as if his eyes fixated, and then emptied of all that was hopeful. Everything that was beautiful.

'No, no. She'll come home.'

He let go of me, stood up, turned away.

'She'll come home, Nahid. She will come home.'

He went into the house with his head bowed and his back bent like an old man.

I sat there. Wondered how we could ever forgive ourselves. How we could ever forgive each other. For bringing Noora with us. For letting her convince us. For enjoying having her with us.

*

What I didn't know and couldn't yet understand was that we too died that day. We were twenty years old, but in so many ways our lives had come to an end. What happened afterwards was just a clumsy attempt to replace what we lost right there, on that day. Our child. Our escape. All my shifts, every hour on the job. All of it.

We should have died that night. All the years that followed were merely borrowed.

You don't leave because you give up. You leave to do something, make something. Build something that's like a middle finger in the face of all the shit that has happened.

People often see me as a victim. They expect me to be weak, submissive. As a refugee woman. I don't understand their thinking. Don't they realise I'm here because I'm strong? That it takes strength not to give up, to refuse to accept misery and oppression? Sometimes I wonder if they think they're strong, that strength comes from never facing hardship. If they think a placid life builds resilience.

I'm proud of my strength. Blow after blow. I get up again every time. Get away every time. Like an immune system, becoming more resistant every time it's attacked. That's how it is! That's just how it is.

But now the cancer has come, and I start to doubt.

'Why did this happen to me?' I ask Christina. The thought bounces around in my head. 'What have I done to deserve this?'

She puts her hand on mine and leans forward. 'It's bad luck, Nahid. It's just bad luck.'

That answer hits me hard. Bad luck. So banal. So provoking. After I fought so hard to have a good life. After being so stubborn, making so many sacrifices.

Bad luck.

Then I realise that it was bad luck that took Noora from us. And luck that I was the one who survived. The same bad luck led my mother not to speak to me for weeks. Bad luck turned me from the pride of my family to its curse.

What if life has nothing to do with strength or weakness? What if it's only chance that steers us? What if I'm just a woman with a lot of bad luck? Maybe that's all I am. In that case, I wish I were weak. I wish I were weak with luck on my side.

It's midsummer. The sun is shining. That's rare, so everyone is happy. I look down from my window. On the grass beneath me preparations are under way. Women in flowery dresses. Children in white. Flower wreaths. And that pole they dance around. It's only ten in the morning, so the festivities haven't really started yet. The people down below are the enthusiasts, there to set everything up. I lean out the window with my chin in my hand watching them. The teacup next to my elbow is dark red. I have a sudden impulse, the kind you get sometimes. I want to lift my cup and tip its hot contents onto their heads. Not because I want to hit them, nor would I actually do it. The thought just passes through my mind and I shudder to myself. Maybe I'm just crazy, maybe this cancer is for the best, both for me and for the world.

My phone beeps. *We'll be there soon, will you come down?*

It's Aram and Johan. They insist I go with them; to me it doesn't matter. I could just as well have stayed at home on the sofa watching TV. But no. I've taken out my flowery dress too.

I put it on and stand in front of the mirror. It's hard to get used to the sight. No hair, no eyebrows. It's like seeing yourself peeled. Faded. It's like I'm disappearing. So I choose a purple scarf, intense purple. I draw on my eyebrows, pressing hard. It's too much, I see that. But I do it anyway. Filling in the contours. I paint my lips. They smear immediately. I sweep my hand over my chin, try to wipe it away, but it's set in the skin. I'll leave it. Better to be too much than to become invisible. Ceasing to exist completely.

I ride the elevator down with my handbag over my arm. I still like it. That feeling of being in motion. Being on my way somewhere. The feeling that it's not over, not completely.

When I open the car door, she turns expectantly. I startle her. She's reacting to my face. I make her uncomfortable. She says nothing, so he turns and speaks instead.

'What a lovely day!'

I nod. 'Yes, we're sure to hear that more than once today.'

He continues smiling, and I want to ask him to stop. I want to tell him that he can't replace my daughter. That she's the one I need.

'How are you feeling, Mama?' she finally asks in a strained voice.

I sigh. Wonder why she asked me to come along if she can't stand me. Why my own daughter looks at me like I'm a monster. Why she can't make me happy. See to it that I'm happy.

'I'm here,' I reply. 'At least that's something.'

They turn away, and the car starts to roll. I see him take her hand, hold it in a tight grip. It makes me sad. Sad that he needs to protect her, comfort her. And that there is nobody sitting next to me to do the same thing, reach for my hand. I'm the one who needs it.

We sit in silence. She turns on Persian music, Googoosh. We drive the same way we've driven so many times before. Down the highway that passes through forests, crosses over bridges and sea. My heart always skips a beat when we do.

To be floating above islands and rocks and cabins and boats and sparkling, clean, clear water. It is such a beautiful place. I have lived here for thirty years, and the beauty is something I never get used to. Such a beautiful place, and I have almost no good memories of it. How could that be?

When she was little, this was what we did together. We got in the car, put on loud music and drove away. We drove out towards Djurö, or past the Värmdö Church, or just out towards Norra Lagnö. My foot pressed a little too hard on the gas. The music was a little too loud. I let go of the wheel and lit another cigarette much too often. I understand now that it wasn't wise. But back then I didn't care. Not even when she was sitting in the car. I was restless. I felt trapped. Yes, I so often felt like a prisoner in my own home, in my own head. Now I'm imprisoned in my sick body.

'Saber is dead,' Masood said one afternoon.

I hadn't heard him come in. He stood in the doorway.

Straight, stiff, almost at attention.

I was sitting on the carpet with Aram on my knee. She was thirteen months old, and the small room we rented wasn't big enough for her to live in. A basement with no windows. A tiny creature can't learn to live like that. She cried and cried, inconsolable. She'd been crying all day. All day we sat on the same spot, and she cried. When he came in, my head was in a fog. I must have been crying too, because I had to blink several times to see him properly. So I asked him to repeat what he'd said. Thought I'd heard wrong, that the syllables had bounced against Aram's anguish and turned into something else in my ears.

'What is wrong with you!' he screamed. 'He's dead. Dead. Dead. Dead. Dead.'

Aram howled even louder. Her tiny hands waved around in the air, as she searched for something to grab onto. Hold fast to. I lifted her up against my chest and hushed her. Hushed her while I tried to think one clear thought, one thought that was anything but emptiness.

'Why are you just sitting there!' he screamed.

I yelled back.

'What am I supposed to do, Masood? What more, what more should we do? It's over, everything's over, there's nothing left.'

He walked over to me and took her in his arms. She cried even louder now. Cried and screamed so it cut into me. It sounded like she couldn't breathe and his eyes were black, darker than I'd ever seen them, and I didn't want him to hold my child.

'Masood, give her to me!'

I was trying to stand upright when a force hit me, hit me so hard that I fell on my back. My first thought was that it must be an earthquake. I thought of Aram. We were in a basement. What if everything collapsed on our heads. Then the force hit me again, and I realised it wasn't coming from the earth, it was coming from him. He stood over me, Aram in his arms, kicking me with his dirty shoes. He kicked at my stomach, my chest, took a run at my face. I raised my arms to protect myself, and he kicked, again and again. I heard tiny bones pop on top of my hands. I heard the loud howl from Aram, my already desperate child. I heard him panting.

And that was where I froze. I lay on the floor, and froze. There were no windows in that room and no phone and I couldn't move. So I lay there, staring down at the pattern on the rug. It was hand-woven. Our most cherished possession. We dragged it with us every time we moved. Masood carried it over his shoulders. I don't know why we thought it was so important to keep. Why that particularly. Hand-woven in deep blue and red with swirling patterns you could drown in. Just like the deep blue of the sea outside the car window bordered by red cabins and green islands creates a swirling pattern you could drown in. It's so beautiful. Why don't I have any good memories?

My child is all that matters to me in this life. It could be because I have so little else. But no matter the reason, that's how it is, all I have is Aram. I love her. I do. Who doesn't love their own child. She's important to me. I want things to go well for her. I want her to be healthy and happy. I want to see her often. I want all of that. But I don't like being a parent. I never have.

When I think of giving birth, one word comes to mind: regret. Regret that I put myself in that situation. Regret that I let my body end up in that state. And the pain. So much pain. Why should anyone have to endure such a thing? Men would never accept it. I was told I should be happy. I was carrying a big baby inside me, who was strong, who thrived. I'd done my job right. I had been pregnant the right way. Now I was supposed to just squeeze it out, this product of my body, this proof I was a good woman. This enormous mass. In my mind I saw someone who didn't want to come out. Someone scratching me with her nails, kicking me with her legs, resisting me with her arms. Someone who was already disappointed with me. Because I spoiled things for her. I pushed her out. Out into this. I imagined she might already hate me.

It was a humiliation. The fluids. The positions I had to contort my body into. They stood me up in bed, pressed my hands against the wall, told me to push. Push, push. Soon a nurse shouted, we see her. Look, look down. I couldn't. I stood there with my cheek against the cold hospital paint, tears running over my swollen breasts, screaming and shaking. And felt regret. Oh, how I felt regret.

When they put her on my chest, I loved her, I did. From the very first moment I loved her. I realised that I would give my life for her. And I guess that was it. I realised I would give my life for her, and that it was impossible to change. It could not be taken back. Now I was she. Now my body existed for her. It scared me. It would mean never-ending torment. She would follow me for the rest of my life.

You can't tell people about feelings like that. Not as a woman, not as a mother. I love my child, but I hate being a mother. I hated it from the first moment. Sometimes I even hate her for putting me into this situation.

When I was diagnosed, my first thought was to call her. I wanted her to stop whatever she was doing. I wanted to scream and cry. I wanted to shout: *Help me. Save me.* I wanted to do that more than anything, but I didn't. I'm proud of myself for that. I chose to protect her, even if only for a few hours.

I've done that so many times in my life. Picked up the phone and asked her to save me. Shouted at her bedroom door: *Help, help me.* I've done it time and time again, to this creature whom I'm supposed to protect, help, rescue. She was there the first time he beat me, and she was with me every time that followed. That's how it was. Neither of us tried to protect her, hide from her eyes the immensity of our failure, all that pain. No, on the contrary.

Once she was at a sleepover with a friend from her soccer team, Malin. Our daughter had a life of her own, even though she was only ten years old. A world of her own. She'd bought crisps and a bag of sweets, all by herself. I dropped her off. I checked to make sure Malin's parents were home.

'You don't need to come in, Mama,' she said.

But I pushed her aside, gently, and stepped inside. In front of the TV, mattresses had been arranged and in the kitchen the table groaned with tacos. Someone had taken such care, someone was going to take good care of her. It tied my stomach in knots.

'You may not go outside after eight o'clock, do you hear me? I don't care what the others are allowed to do, or if they do it anyway, you will not!'

She nodded, looked away. She wanted to get rid of me.

She wanted to go into that other world, her own world.

'I'll call and check on you!'

She nodded again. She would go out, I knew that. She would do whatever she felt like. As I would have done.

Then I walked home through that summer evening. Swedish summer. I love it. It was warm and green between the terraced houses. The air held the scent of that little forest lake. Damp, warm, green. I walked slowly, didn't hurry home. I was in absolutely no rush to get home. He was there. He wasn't working that evening, and I wasn't working, and she would be sleeping somewhere else. Leaving us alone. I went into the empty playground, sat down on a swing and gave myself a push. I think I stayed there a long time. Swinging back and forth, higher and higher, faster and faster, then I rested a bit. Stared out over the neighbourhood. It was a luxury for us to live there. Not that we didn't deserve it, we did. We'd worked hard to get there. But mostly because it was such a contrast to where we started.

I will never forget the night we moved into our first apartment on Nelson's Hill. We came straight from the refugee camp. We were ready to start our new life. But that neighbourhood ... it didn't look anything like what we'd seen of Sweden so far. It looked like something on the margins. On the border between Sweden and I don't know what. Maybe emptiness. Not in some magical, fairy-tale way. The refugee camp had been like that. Charming little cottages in the woods. We had to share with another family, but it didn't matter. It was so beautiful. This. This was asphalt and concrete and steel, and long rows of dirty green balconies shared by several apartment doors. It was ugly. It stank of urine. Drunks swayed between the buildings. There were screams coming from inside the apartments.

What could we do? We were in a land where peace and democracy and freedom prevailed. But it was also horrible. Nelson's Hill: landing there showed us clearly that we were at the bottom. There was us, the political refugees. And there were the drunks and the single mothers and all the others who'd been living in peace and democracy their whole lives, but who'd made it no further than this. We didn't want to be there. And we didn't plan to stay there any longer than we had to. So we worked. And worked. Worked, made money, and squirrelled it away. Wore old, ragged clothes and were stingy at the dinner table. And then we bought the terraced house. Moved our few belongings to a nice quiet place.

You try. You try to build something good, because it's better than the alternative. And you think you can, think you have the ability to create something beautiful. But it doesn't happen. It's not as good as it should be. Not as good as the image you had of it, as what you'd hoped. I don't know. I still struggle to understand. You think if you've managed to escape a war and find your way to peace, you should be so much happier. If you've lived with your infant in a basement, with bombs falling above you, and now you have a garden and the sky is clear, you should be happier. You think maybe if you didn't have to live surrounded by drunkards and police sirens, you'd be happier. But it doesn't work that way, and I don't know why.

I went home finally. Gently opened the door. I glanced at the clock on the wall and realised I'd been gone a long time. Too long. It was quiet in the apartment, an ominous silence. I was expecting at least the drone of a soccer game coming from the TV. But not a sound, not a movement. I walked towards the bathroom door. Thought I'd take a shower, kill some time. Then it came.

'Come here!'

Masood's voice was harsh, and I obeyed. He was sitting on the sofa in the living room. Staring into space.

'Where have you been?' he asked.

'I dropped off Aram, you know that.'

'That was two hours ago! Where have you been for the last two hours?'

'I took a walk. Around the neighbourhood. It's a lovely evening.'

'You haven't been walking!' Now he was on his feet. 'Who were you with? Tell me.'

What if I could have done something else in those moments, said something else, would it have stopped there? If I'd put my hand on his arm and said: *My love. I'm sorry. I should have hurried. I was wrong.* What if I'd said those words. Stretched up and kissed him. Would that have made a difference? Would everything have changed then, our whole lives? If I'd done that, maybe he would have lived. Maybe I wouldn't be dying. Would it have been worth it? To sacrifice my pride. I'm not sure.

'What business is it of yours? I can see who I want, when I want!'

That is what I said instead, and he raised his hand above my head. I screamed, expecting her to come to my rescue. But she didn't come. She wasn't there.

*

When a man beats a woman, he can do it in so many ways. If you haven't experienced it personally, you probably think it consists of a slap to the face. A shove into a wall. But he did so much more. It was as if his anger was endless and once awakened it could not be stopped. And the sounds, if only you'd recorded the sounds. Collected the fluids. The odour. There were screams, usually not many words, mostly just screams. Just my sobs, my tears. Just his panting, his sweat. It was hot tea hitting the wallpaper. It was cigarettes smoked in the pauses. And then the sound of blows.

Most often it started that way, with a raised hand and a smack across the face. Sometimes it was a slap, but usually a closed fist. A fist to my mouth. Across my cheek. To my forehead. Under my chin. It varied. The first blow was enough, really. I usually fell from that. He could have been satisfied with that, but that's not how it worked. He started kicking me as I lay there. Kicking my legs, stomach and breasts if he could. I'd quickly curl into a foetal position, and he'd move on to my back. Not my head, not how I remember it, anyway. But now and then I fainted, an early blow was so hard that it knocked me out. I think that scared him. He'd usually fetch a pitcher of cold water and pour it over me. Then it would be over. If I was knocked out early, I'd escape the worst of it. The hunt. The hunt was the worst. Being hunted down by the man I slept next to at night.

When he kicked me, I tried to get up and run away. I managed often enough. He wasn't exactly a professional boxer. I don't think he'd been in many fights other than with me. So he kicked and waved his arms around without knowing what he was doing. When I ran, he ran after me. Once he grabbed a hockey stick in the hall and beat me down with it. Once he caught up with me and put his hands around my neck, pressed me against the bed frame and started to strangle me.

I thought I was going to die that time. So did she. Those who hear this may wonder: Dear God, where was the child? Well, she was right there! Between us.

When he ran after me with the hockey stick, he struck her down first. Not on purpose. He was never after her. But she was in the way. She could tell by looking at him when the first blow was on its way. She stood between us. Fell onto the rug as he pushed her aside. And that day, the day I thought he was going to strangle me to death, she was there. She pulled at his arms, pushed his body. Screamed: *Stop, stop!* But it had no effect, so she ran away. I heard her run, heard her slam the front door. She'll get help, I thought. But nothing happened. Everything went black. And when I woke up I was lying in bed, alone. The room was dark. No sound could be heard. I tried to clear my throat, straining to wheeze out the words. When I finally succeeded, I said her name.

'Aram! Aram!' I whispered at first, but finally the terror poured out in my voice.

'Araaam, Araaam.' I screamed and screamed and screamed.

Soon I heard the front door open and then the bedroom door. She stuck her head in. Curls wild, eyes wide.

'Help me,' I said, and she came forward. Sank down on the floor. Took my hand in one of hers and stroked my hair with the other.

'Why did you leave me?' was what I said to her. Not, everything will be all right. Not, I'm sorry. None of the things a mother should say. I was just angry. Angry at her.

'Why did you leave me.'

*

That summer night. When she'd escaped to the sleepover, to the idyllic world someone else had built for her. When I walked home slowly, swinging in the empty playground, staring at the terraced houses and the small garden plots that belonged to people who had neither too much, nor too little. When I came home to silence, and he was waiting for me, and I answered back, and he stood up and knocked me down. Then it was as if we were both missing something. Our flow was disrupted. I lay on the floor, he stood over me, and I cried.

'I want to go and get Aram,' I said. And he agreed.

I don't remember how he put it, but he let me get up and go. I got in the car and drove the few minutes to where she was staying. It was after I'd rung the doorbell that I first caught my reflection in the window and for a moment I wondered what I was doing. My makeup was running, my ponytail drooped, and my cheek was a burning red. When the door opened, I was quick to raise my hand to cover it. Hide the flames on my face. I had hoped that one of the children would answer the door, but it was not to be, of course. It was the mother, the woman who lived there.

'Oh, hello,' she said hesitantly.

'I'm here to pick up Aram,' I said.

She shook her head, as if it were her decision. 'Oh, but they're having so much fun.'

I swallowed hard.

'I understand. But she needs to come home.'

I saw the way she looked at me. She didn't want to move out of the way. But she realised it wasn't her right to resist.

'Has something happened?' she asked.

I didn't answer.

I just said 'Can you go and get her?'

She looked at me, a long look. I don't know if she was judging me or feeling sorry for me. But she went inside. I heard the sound of happy voices, heard them being interrupted. Saw five girls come towards me in the hall. Staring at me. With the same expression as the mother, or so I thought, but what did they know. Then she came. Her things packed, a backpack in hand. She didn't look at me. She didn't look at her friends, either. She just said goodbye straight into the air and walked out. Walked past me.

Maybe pain moves in a circle, maybe I caused her pain to avenge my own.

When she was little, I'd put her in the car and just drive. Those are probably the best memories I gave her, even if they were rooted in my anxiety. Maybe she didn't notice, maybe she saw only energy. The energy I conjured up to escape from what pursued me. We drove through green meadows and thick forests and over sparkling water. The archipelago entranced us, even though we were living in the middle of it. We mostly listened to Persian music. Googoosh. Just like now, driving with Johan on our way to see his family. I like that she's playing the same music around him. That she shows off what I've given her.

Man o to ba hamim ama delamon kheyli doore. We sit so close to each other, but our hearts are far apart. When she was little, she looked at me with wide eyes while I sang. She liked it, I could see that, and it made me sing even louder. Sometimes she asked me to turn off the stereo and sing other songs, ones that weren't on cassette or CD. The folk songs of my childhood. She knew a few lines, sang along. She didn't understand the words, the strange dialect, but somehow she knew what they meant. I saw it on her face. Or maybe she was just mimicking me unconsciously. My loss, my grief. Such things are handed down as sure as the raven-black hair.

We felt protected in the car. Protected by metal and by speed. The two of us were protected without having to protect each other. And the music, it was our link to the outside. It tied us to where we came from. She probably felt that, too. This was the music she came from. I think, in some strange way, she feels closer to those songs than to the glittering archipelago. Maybe that will be the case for as long as I exist. Maybe she'll finally be free from them, too, when I die. Maybe then she'll be able to move her roots to the islands and the sea instead.

But now it's midsummer, and somebody else is driving the car. A person she's found, from her world. I'm sitting in the back seat, protected from nothing. Everything has caught up with me now and nothing in the world moves fast enough for me to escape.

We arrive at the water and park the car. This is where our car rides used to end. I drove and drove until we reached the water. Then we sat and looked at the sea for a few minutes, until I turned and drove the other way, and we reached water again. But today we're being picked up by boat. Today the world stretches a little further. Johan's father helps me aboard and everyone stares at me, as if I might break at any moment. Don't worry about me, I want to say. I'll be fine. But I stay silent. Thinking of how my insides are being devoured and broken down, becoming more and more crushed by the hour.

The motorboat probably isn't going that fast, but it feels like it to me. I hold on tight, close my eyes, and let the wind whip me. Whip against my skin, through the scarf around my head and against my bare skull. I hear nothing but the wind and the engine and I like it. It makes me feel alive, more alive than I have felt in a long time.

'Thank you,' I say to his father as the boat slows down.

I try to say it so he understands. But he thinks I'm thanking him for the ride.

'Of course,' he says. Only that, of course.

Perhaps it's not possible to understand that someone is thanking you for life, if you are not also about to die.

My father was ill for as long as I can remember. He lay on his bed in the kitchen to be close to us, to be among us. Next to him stood a tray, always with a burning hookah and a glass of tea. He had opium, his painkiller, in a water pipe. No medication, no complaints. I used to lie down next to him and listen to his stories. His thoughts. He had so many thoughts about life. On a level that I didn't really understand. He was a Sufi, a dervish. I didn't know what that meant. I thought a dervish was a beggar who knocked on your door, who read you prayers in exchange for food and a place to sleep for the night. Sometimes they told children stories about dervishes to frighten them. If you don't eat up, the dervish will take you! I thought that couldn't be what my father was.

My uncle used to call him the philosopher, and I suppose that was more how it was. He talked about life and love. About our love for him and his love for the earth. About the beauty in lifting a handful of sand and watching it slip through your fingers and seek the ground. I didn't understand much of what he said, but the image of the sand stuck with me. I used to squat outside our door, lifting handfuls of yellow sand and slowly watching it fall back to the ground.

'Why are you getting your hands dirty!' my mother cried when she saw me.

When I replied that it was because of what my father had said, she rolled her eyes and slammed the door. Her world was in the everyday. Cooking, working, cleaning. But my father's world, that was something else:

> Sand streams down to the earth because that's where it belongs. We can lift it, capture it, transport it. But even after oceans of time pass by, even after we've carried it across thousands of miles, sand will seek the earth again when the opportunity arises. So we are all bound to our origins.

If my life had turned out differently maybe I'd remember something else of all the things my father told me. But those are the words I think about.

I wander away to the little beach, while everyone else stays seated around the midsummer table on the dock. The white sand isn't natural, it's been brought here. Transported across the sea to this tiny island. I sit with my legs pulled up, my red toenails pushed beneath the surface. I gently lift a fistful, embracing it, holding tight. Maybe you can defy it, maybe you can make things stay put even where they don't belong. The sand in the air, in my hand. I squeeze so hard my hand cramps. Then I let go with a groan.

'Is everything OK?' Aram calls from the dock.

I nod. The sand has fallen back to the earth.

This is an island, and they own it. A piece of land that rises straight out of the sea, and they own it. I marvel at that. Apart from the sand on the beach, which has been brought here, everything on the island is sturdy and solid. As if nothing could shake it. There are trees across most of it, towering trees. Trunks so wide they block your view. I marvel at them, at things that are left in peace. When you walk down the paths, roots crisscross under your feet. I feel them with my hands. They can't be lifted, can't be forced to go anywhere else. They'll never slip through any fingers, never fall to the earth seeking home again. They're already there, will always be there. I look out at the people sitting around their midsummer feast.

Think, I'm a people of sand, and they are a people of roots.

When the time came for me to start school, my mother told me I was moving in with Maryam. She worked in a small town three hours away, and I would be in her class, become her student. In the evenings, I was supposed to help out around the house. Cooking, cleaning, that sort of thing. It still makes me angry to think of my mother sending me away. Sending me off to relieve the burden on my sister. It makes me angry because I was used. Like a tool. I wasn't treated as something with intrinsic value, not as something to cherish.

Maryam had been married that summer. Her husband was also named Masood, I suppose it was just the irony of fate. There were not as many liberal men available as there were women in my family. So, often we were stuck with assholes. Masood was a teacher like Maryam and a year younger than her. I think that's where the problem started. My sister was more than him. Better at mathematics, the subject they both taught. Better with people: he was constantly ending up in conflicts, and she had to step in to solve them. Besides, she was beautiful, proud, strong. Everything a woman can't be, not even in Sweden, without getting shit for it. So he pushed her down. He forbade her to work in the evenings. She was supposed to cook, tend to their home, wash his clothes. And while he was working, she had to sit next to him, sewing holes in his shirts and polishing his shoes. That's how things were, just like that. And so I was needed, to help wait on him. To keep her company in the kitchen after he'd screamed at her, and she'd retreated. As a kind of shield. At least that's what they thought I'd be.

It was impossible for a teacher not to work in the evenings. She needed to mark exams and plan her assignments. So she slipped out of bed after he'd fallen asleep, lit a dim light far from the bedroom, usually in the entrance hall. And there she sat, with her piles of papers, glasses on her nose and pen in her mouth. Her mahogany hair was piled in a high bun on her head and her long neck and thick eyelashes made her look like a fairy in the dim light. Beautiful, beautiful. She was so beautiful.

I lay on a mattress in the living room, like a watchdog. The entire spectacle played out before my eyes. She followed him into the bedroom. In the best case, their voices were low, a few words exchanged before it went quiet. Then a few minutes later the sound of his snores. The creak of the bedsprings. And she pattered by me on tiptoe. She went into the kitchen where she hid her bag in a kitchen cabinet. Took out what she needed. Sat down at her place. Looked in my direction and winked.

'Sleep now, *azizam*.' My love.

I smiled, blew her a kiss. Closed my eyes and listened to the sound of her pen strokes until they rocked me to sleep.

And then everything changed. Everything changed, and it was my fault. The winter was harsh that year and we weren't used to snow and cold, not like that. I came home from school one day with a fever and a cough that rattled my whole body. I was seven years old, as thin as a leaf, and far away from my mother. I didn't want to make trouble, so I huddled in my corner of the living room and tried to be still, tried to be quiet. But my body was boiling and vibrating, and I just couldn't make myself invisible. I think I was the first thing he saw when he got home. My wet, shivering body. He didn't want me there.

He was very particular about cleanliness. Refused to take someone's hand if he didn't know it was newly washed. He wanted Maryam to rinse all the fruit and vegetables with soap. She had to take out the rugs and scrub them in the sun every Friday. She cleaned the bathroom every night and every morning. Sometimes he opened the door, stuck his head in, and checked. Then he shouted her name. *Maryam!* Such a soft name said in the harshest tone of voice. He was displeased every time he checked.

I think he actually liked having me live there. He liked seeing her with a child at her side in the kitchen. But when I was sick, he didn't want me around, and I had nowhere else to go. I could see that it made her stressed. She put me in the bathroom. Let the hot water run for as long as it lasted, and then told me to remain there in the steam. 'It's good for your lungs,' she said and left. But I knew she just wanted to get me out of his way.

'The girl will make me sick, Maryam. This won't do.'

I sat on the small plastic stool in the bathroom, listening to their voices.

'Don't worry, Masood. It's just one night. I won't let her touch anything. It will pass.'

'Shouldn't I be able to relax in my own home? Do I need to worry about germs and shit inside my own walls?'

'She's a child. Please. It won't hurt us, it will pass.'

'Now you're late with dinner! Because you've been taking care of the girl. She's supposed to be here to help!'

'Please. Of course. She helps me. She will help me tomorrow. It's not a problem.'

There was silence, and I knew she was hurrying into the kitchen. I pictured her, sitting on the rug in front of the stove. Rocking back and forth as she stirred her pots, like an old woman. It was the anxiety. She was completely on edge. As if she were waiting for an order. A complaint. The sound of her name, of her name flung like an accusation. Or else she knew. Maybe she knew it was coming that night. Maybe I was the only one who was surprised.

The heat and steam in the bathroom began to subside, but I didn't dare move. I sat there. Shivering. I heard him leafing through his papers. Heard her throw the oilcloth on the rug. Set out plates and cutlery. I heard them sit down and start eating. I knew she wasn't coming to get me. My fingernails had turned blue and my cough cut into my chest. I turned on the water. Hoped it would be hot again, but it was still freezing. I turned off the tap and sat down. My whole body shook and my head was spinning with fever. I didn't know what to do. I just wanted to go home to my mother. I wanted to go home to the kitchen floor and lie beside my father's bedside and listen to his stories. About the earth and love. Love.

I remember that I became angry, angry with my sister. I remember that feeling overtaking me. I got up and opened the bathroom door. Naked and coughing, I ran out. Maryam and Masood both looked up from their plates in surprise. I think we were all shocked by what I dared to do. We stood there looking at each other, and no one said anything. I ran towards my drawer in the corner of the living room. I was standing with my back to them, and I dug out my towel, tried to find my clothes. The cough made my eyes fill with tears, and I saw nothing. At that moment, I stood in my own fog, frozen by the fear of what I'd done.

Behind me was only silence. Stillness and silence. Then I heard him stand up, throw his spoon down on his plate and walk towards the entrance hall. He put on his coat and slammed the door behind him. I didn't dare turn around. I pulled on my pants with trembling hands. Pulled a long-sleeved shirt over my head. Took out my mattress, which was curled up next to the bureau, grabbed my blanket and pillow out of the bottom drawer. I made my bed and lay down, keeping my back to my sister. She hadn't risen from her seat. Not a sound had escaped her. I felt ashamed. Ashamed of what I'd done to her. I figured I hadn't had any choice, but I knew she hadn't either.

I dozed and woke up hours later to a thump. I sat up abruptly. The room was in darkness. Now I heard a thud, and another thump. It was coming from the bedroom. I ran to the door, put my ear against it and listened. The muffled explosions came one after the other, but they were the only sounds. Thumps and deep breaths. Gasps. I pushed cautiously on the door, peeked through the crack. She lay on the floor, facing away from me. He stood over her, kicking his hard foot against her soft belly. She lay still, silent. I wanted to scream, but held back. Closed the door gently, and lay down on my mattress. Drowned my cough in my pillow. She was dead, I was sure of it. He had killed her, and maybe he would come for me next.

A minute later the bedroom door was thrown open, and I heard him pass by. Walked to the front hall and disappeared into the night. I quickly got to my feet and ran, threw myself on the floor next to her.

'Maryam, Maryam, Maryam!'

She didn't answer. Her eyes were closed, her cheeks red, yellow, almost blue. I put my finger under her nose, as you do with a sleeping baby to make sure it's breathing. I felt nothing at first, but then it came. Weak, but it was there. She was alive. I got up again and went into the kitchen, filled a bowl with cold water and took the tea towel from the hook. In the living room, I hesitated. Thought maybe I should lock the front door, buy us some peace. A little time. But the image of his rage was too fresh. I didn't dare. I ran back to Maryam instead. Dipped the towel in cold water and bathed her forehead, her cheeks, her eyes. The cold water mixed with drops of sweat that fell from my feverish face and the tears running down my neck.

'Open your eyes,' I whispered. 'Please, Maryam, open your eyes.'

Somehow she woke up in the end. Gazed up at me with those beautiful green eyes. We looked at each other silently. Then she took the towel from my hand and dipped it into the bowl. She lifted her arm with a groan and wiped my fevered brow, and I curled up and lay down close to her, and there we lay for the rest of the night. Neither of us slept, we just lay huddled together staring straight ahead. Watchfully. Waiting for him to come back.

When I was home over the New Year holiday, I told my father about Maryam and her husband. I told him how he tormented her. And how she only responded with more care. I wanted Papa to talk to her. Tell her to yell back. Tell her to move on.

I was lying on the carpet with my head in his lap, as he slowly twirled his pipe between his fingers.

'It is a higher thing to love than to be loved, *dokhtaram*.'

I looked at him incredulously. Was that all? Wasn't he going to defend our honour? Wasn't he going to protect Maryam?

He glanced at my mother, standing at the stove, and I understood even though I was just a child. Mama's tense, slender back. Her unsmiling face. I understood that he loved her without being loved back. And I knew then that was not what I wanted. I knew I wanted to be loved, that I wanted to feel it every moment. To do the loving, that was nothing but work and disappointment.

One day Aram shows me an article. I roll my eyes. Another thing she actually wants to share with Masood. But I'm the only one here. The only one left. And soon she'll have nobody. Poor kid.

How could we have done this to her. Our little bundle who was our entire world, who was meant to replace all the worlds that had disappeared. What if we had known. What if we had known it would end up like this. That we would tear her from our roots and our families, take her far away, and then die. Abandon her. Leave her alone in a country that wasn't hers. Because it's not. No matter how Swedish she's become. There is no one here to take care of her, not like she would have been taken care of if we'd stayed. We did this to her.

I wonder now what's worth more. Freedom and democracy. Or people who love you. People who will take care of your children when you die.

The article is about someone who died. It makes me angry when I realise that. Why would she show me something like that? Why doesn't she try to protect me? *I don't want to die!* I want to yell at her. *Why are you showing me death?*

It's about Kiarostami. The director. Masood's idol. Cancer,

just like me. It's comforting somehow. I can't say that to her, but it's my first thought. I'm not the only one facing death with no hair, without my own body or my dignity. No one is safe. Despite talent. Despite fame. Despite money. In the face of cancer, we are all equal.

'I wasn't prepared for everything to end so quickly,' she says.

Her voice is rough. I hear how she's trying to push it down. Push it away.

'I thought we'd get more time. More time before it was over. Before everyone was gone. Before it all . . . It was going to turn out OK in the end, Mama. Turn out good. For Dad. For you.'

Now she's crying. Not quietly, but like a child. She sobs and snot runs from her nose.

'I don't understand why it has to end like this! Why we never got to have it good. Never got any peace. He was supposed to feel better! I thought he'd be allowed to feel better! And now he's gone.'

She lies on her stomach on the sofa now, her face buried in her arms. I scoot over. Stroke her hair.

'Cry it out,' I say. 'Cry it out, darling. What else can you do. Cry, cry.'

I feel her body relax. She lets go of some part of what she's carrying inside. Something opens up in her. I continue to stroke her hair.

'I don't understand why everything disappears, Mama. Why everyone disappears. I don't understand it. Don't know how to do this. There will be nothing left. It feels like I'm hovering in mid-air. I just don't understand why everything has to keep disappearing.'

I lift my hand from her. I don't mean to do it, but it's as if I can't let it linger. I want her to cry. I want her to grieve.

I want her to mourn me. I don't want her to feel sorry for herself. Grieve for her own destiny. She is the one receiving the fruit of all our labours. Of all our losses. She inherits everything we hoped for, and all the things we took for granted. Freedom. Possibilities. Life. She is the one who gets to live. And here she is. Feeling sorry for herself.

Everything disappears, I want to say to her. All worlds. All people. You are a child of war. You are a refugee. You ought to know that. Did you think it only applied to other people? Did you think we left it behind? That it's something you can escape? Read a history book! Nothing endures. Everything will disappear and the world will become another. That's what you come from. That's the blood that flows in your veins. It will take generations to replace it. Generations before thousands of years of war, rebellion and chaos are replaced by Swedish peace. Swedish constancy.

'That's how it is,' I say simply. My tone is harsh, but I let it be. 'As long as I can remember, everything has disappeared. As long as you live, you'll experience the same thing.'

*

But when she's gone, I stand by the window with the article in my hand. It's from the Internet. She's printed it out and brought it here. For my sake. For her sake, because it was important to her. She wanted to talk about it. She wanted some form of comfort from me. Because Kiarostami is dead. I look at the paper in my hand, at the blurry image. I read the words. They're in English but I understand:

> A tree is rooted in the ground. If you transfer it from one place to another, the tree will no longer bear fruit. If I had left my country, I would be the same as the tree.

It hits me like a fist in the stomach. I didn't know. I didn't realise that was so. That that is how it would be. That there was so much that would disappear. Here I am thinking she ought to understand, but I didn't for such a long time. Only now do I understand.

I was standing by the window in my apartment. It was dark and cold outside. This was before the cancer. Before all this. And to think I thought I was unhappy then. My jacket hung on my shoulders, the tea glass was cradled in my hands, and each breath rose in the darkness. One after the other. Evenly. My mobile rang next to me on the window ledge. It was Aram. I decided not to answer. I wanted to stay there a moment longer. Drink my tea. Take a sleeping pill and go to bed. Stay in my own world. I also thought, I really did, that I didn't want to answer. I feel that way sometimes when she calls. I don't want to answer, don't want to give her the satisfaction of having reached me. I want her to think of me more than she does. I want to be in her head the rest of the evening, want her to wonder how I'm doing. I want her to think: *I have to call Mama again.* So I didn't answer the first time, but she called again. I looked at the phone, almost let it go to voicemail. But at the last second I picked it up. I heard the sound of the subway, clattering.

'Call me when it's not so noisy!' That was the first thing I said.

She was quiet. I think she wanted to hang up when she heard me. Heard my tone of voice. Heard my words. She must have thought there was no help to be had from me.

'Hello, hello, are you still there? I can't hear you.'

She decided to try anyway.

'Something terrible's happened, Mama,' she said.

I don't know why, but it didn't move me. It should have moved me. I should have been worried. I should have been frightened. I should have had some kind of reaction. But I didn't. Nothing at all.

'OK. What?'

All I heard was the subway rumbling in my ear. So I went on.

'We'll talk tomorrow. I'll call you tomorrow.'

I hung up. Looked out into the darkness again. Across the lake, into the woods. What could possibly be so horrible. It was probably nothing.

I had closed the window and was headed for bed when she called back. I remember I sighed. Rolled my eyes. But I picked up the phone again. I did. I was probably going to say something that would have made things even worse. But I didn't have time.

'Dad died. Dad is dead.'

She must have been in a quiet tunnel. It was like an echo. *Dad is dead. Dad is dead.* I don't know if she said anything more. I don't know if I said anything more. I don't remember.

I only know that I was thinking: We didn't escape. We didn't escape. We, who didn't want to die. We, who just didn't want to die.

I know she's in the room. I know she found me. A neighbour must have called her and told her an ambulance picked me up. She probably called around to all the A&Es. And she found me, and she came here. I don't have the energy to open my eyes, but I know she's sitting at the foot of the bed. On a stool, leaning forward. She never sits in the padded chairs with backrests. She never leans back. No, I know she's sitting there leaning forward, watching over me.

I hear the birds chirp outside. Feel the warm breeze coming through the open window caress my body. I know she's wearing a tank top and wide-legged pants and high heels. I can hear her heels tap against the floor. She does so quietly, gently, but she can't help herself. She is anxious, restless. She doesn't want me to live any longer. She wants me to just get it over with and die. So it's done. So the torment will end. For me and for her.

Why can't I just die. I wish I would. My body is numb. I try to move, turn on my side, but I have no control. I hear her get up, her metal stool scraping against the floor. She's noticed my attempt to move. She takes my hand.

'Mama,' she says. 'Mama, I'm here. I'm here, Mama. I won't leave you.'

Her voice trembles, breaks. 'Mama. Mama. Mama.'

She falls down on the floor beside the bed, holding my hand between hers.

She starts singing, quietly quietly.

Man o ba khodet bebar, man ba raftan hazeram.

It's Googoosh again. I try to squeeze her hand, but mine won't comply. It won't listen. It lies flat and motionless. It's already dead in hers.

I want to ask her to stop. Not that one. She won't die, she won't follow me anywhere. She'll live, she'll live a long time. I want to make her understand that. That if she doesn't, everything is lost. She falls silent. Or maybe I fall asleep.

When I open my eyes, the rain is beating against the window. It must be a new day. She's sitting in a big sweater, with sneakers on her feet. Her face is bare, her hair in a messy bun.

'Why do you look like that,' I say in a croaking voice. 'Don't you dress up for your mother?'

She lets out a laugh. A short one. As you do when something isn't funny, but there's no better way to respond. She calls for the nurse and sits down next to me.

'How are you feeling, Mama?'

The lump in my throat is about to explode. I want to scream. Scream! Call for help. Give a piece of my mind to whatever brought me here. Just scream. But my mouth is dry, and I can't. I shake my head. She presses my hand. Looks away, out the window at the rain beating, beating down.

It's the chemo. It's breaking me down. I have a high fever and some kind of infection. Antibiotics are being pumped into my blood intravenously. Antibiotics and God knows what else. I lie there connected to tube after tube, and I don't know a thing. Can't do a thing.

'I'm a nurse, too,' I say when the nurse comes in to take my blood pressure and check my pulse. I want the person sticking needles into my bruised and busted arm to know that. I want her to know that I understand these things. I'm an equal. Not just a victim, a wretch in her care. She smiles.

'Lovely!' That's all she says.

She gathers her things, whistling, pushes her cart in front of her and waves goodbye.

'The doctor will be here soon.'

Aram stares after her emptily. It might be a long time until Aram is whistling again, I think. It might be a long time before something feels lovely. It occurs to me that I'm sinking and dragging her down with me.

'She must have a date,' I say. Trying to look happy. Aram turns to me, startled. It takes a moment, but then she smiles back, and I feel my smile become genuine in return.

'Maybe there's some handsome old man with prostate cancer around here who wants to get a coffee with me.' Aram laughs and the sound of her laughter causes a flutter in my stomach.

'I saw one in the corridor who looks like Mikael Persbrandt . . . a Persbrandt with no hair.'

She winks at me.

'I'd rather wait for the real one.'

We sit smiling at each other for a while. Without moving, without words. Like a couple of idiots, we smile at each other until I get too tired and turn away.

*

When Christina enters she looks worried.

'We're going to have to put the chemo on hold,' she says.

'What does that mean?' Aram asks. 'What do we do instead?'

'Nothing,' she replies. 'Her body isn't strong enough right now.'

'So she gets no treatment? We just let the cancer spread freely?'

'That risk exists,' Christina replies. 'But otherwise the chemo will kill her. I'm very sorry.'

She leaves us and the pouring rain pours down even more. We both stare at the window. The fury flying against the glass. Hitting it. Running down. Aram has sat down at the small desk with a pen in her hand. She's scratching away at something. Drawing, I would guess, but my ears hear only the scratching.

'Stop it!' I say. I must have screamed, because she looks at me in surprise. 'If it's so boring to be here, you might as well leave.'

Her dark dark eyes. She looks at me like a child. A hurt and overwrought child. My little kid.

'Leave. It's for the best. I'm tired. I need to sleep. Go.'

She sits still, as though paralysed.

'See you tomorrow, if you have time. There is nothing to be done. You heard it yourself.'

Aram gathers her things quickly. She must have been longing to go, longing to be released.

'In a hurry?' I ask, and she stiffens.

'Do you want me to stay, Mama? I'll stay as long as you want.'

She's lying, I think. *If that were true, she would never leave.*

It feels like I spent the rest of my life in that hospital. I had a 104-degree fever, and nothing could get it down. I hallucinated. I suppose that's what it was. Hallucinations. Whatever those are. Aren't we hallucinating all the time? Seeing the world through our own cloudy filters. Do we ever experience anything real? Actually for real? Cancer. I suppose that's real. But at the same time not. Why did I start chemo in the first place? When they said you're going to die. Why didn't I just take my money and run? I could have got pretty far, lived in luxury. I could have brought Aram with me. We could have gone to Hawaii, drunk huge cocktails on lounge chairs, had massages every day. We could have gone to New York and stayed in five-star hotels. We could have travelled to Las Vegas and gambled at a casino. When the end was close, I could have said goodbye to her. Sent her home. With hugs and kisses and my mind intact. And then I'd buy an old convertible and drive down to Texas, into the desert. I'd have found a mountain and driven to the top. I'd have drunk a bottle of brandy and smoked a pack of cigarettes and dangled my legs over the edge, drinking, smoking, singing. And then I'd have got in my car, put my foot on the gas, thrown my arms in the air, screamed, and driven. The car would have lifted up off the ground, floated in the air. I would have flown. I would have screamed and flown, and life would have been its most beautiful just as it ended.

That is what I could have done. Burned the candle at both ends. Lived until I felt satisfied. Finished. But I missed my chance.

They said: You have cancer. You will die. And I chose to fight death instead of squeezing the last out of life. I don't really know why I chose this path. But I would probably choose it again, if given the choice. I realise that. I realise I'm more afraid of dying than not living well. I think I've always been like that. That's who I was in the interrogation room. That's why I betrayed everything, betrayed it all, and turned into a traitor. And I'm like that in this hospital room. More afraid to die than of not living all the way. If that's not delusional, I don't know what delusion is.

The infection has subsided, and I'll be discharged soon. I don't want to leave. I don't want to go home and be alone. Yes, it's that simple. I like it better in the hospital. Better to be in the company of the dying and their weary nurses than in my own home. Plus people come to the hospital to visit, because when someone's in the hospital you have to visit them. Once I'm home, they'll think I can get by on my own. So I want to stay.

I said as much to Christina. I don't feel strong enough yet. She took my hand and sat down on the chair next to me, which they rarely do. Most often they just stand above you looking down. She took my hand and spoke to me in a gentle voice.

'I understand. But I'm afraid that this is the way it is now. You will never feel strong enough.'

I want to raise my hand, with all the tubes and needles attached to it, and slap her across the face. A slap that would make her head rattle, blacken her eyes. What kind of thing is that to say to somebody. How could you send another human being out into the world with those words. *I'm stronger than you think*, I want to say to her. But it won't help, because then she'd put me in the first hospital transport vehicle and send me home. And besides, I don't even know if it's true.

I always believed it, always thought so, that I'm stronger than people think. But now it's the other way around. People see me as a survivor, but they're wrong. I'm so scared, I'm so afraid of death. More scared than I've ever been, more frightened than I ever thought I could be. I thought death would hit hard and fast. A bullet in the head, a car accident, a slap, a bang and then the end. That's what I was prepared for. Not this. The waiting. And waiting. It's been a year now since I was diagnosed, since they told me I would die. A year and I may have at least that much time left. A year of waking up each morning to the idea: I'm dying. And one day, one day very soon, I will.

This was not what I imagined. What I expected from life. This protracted wait for death.

We're going to a concert, Aram said. She bought the tickets and made the plans. I don't know why, what gave her the idea. She has some picture in her head of us doing things together, before I disappear. Beautiful things. But I don't know if I'm up for it, between the struggle with tumours and toxins. I don't know if I want to.

'You can do it, Mama,' she says. 'You can come with me.'

She knows that Christina is discharging me. She's happy about it. She thinks that means there's hope.

What do you know, I want to say. What do any of you know about what's happening inside me.

'We'll take a taxi the whole way. And we'll take a taxi back. You only have to walk a few dozen metres. It's no big deal, you can do it.'

You can do it. Like I'm a two-year-old she's trying to get onto the potty.

'I don't want to,' I say. 'It's my last night in the hospital. I want to be here.'

'But the concert is tonight, Mama. Only tonight. I can't change that. And who knows if . . . '

'Who knows what!' I get mad at her. 'Who knows if there will be another chance? Who knows if I'll die tomorrow?'

She bites her lip like she does when she's hurt. I know it,

but she thinks she's keeping it inside. I see her emotions as clearly as I see the moon shining on winter nights. Clearly, clearly. Hide it better, I want to say to her. You're not doing it well enough. I don't want to see everything you feel, don't you know that. I feel enough as it is. And I don't want you laying any more guilt and shame on me with your eyes. Are you hurt? Are you? I don't care, because I'm dying. I will die, and you will live. Do you understand? I can do whatever I want to you.

'Just go!' is all I say. 'I'm not coming.'

She lowers her tense shoulders and walks out. I squeeze the turquoise, patterned pillow she bought for me. Close my eyes and dry my tears in the fabric.

Christina knocks on the door, sticks her head in. Again. For the second time today. I just want to be left alone.

'Do you really have this level of resources?' I ask. 'What have I done to deserve so much attention?'

Then I remember where I am and what's going on and sit up in bed.

'Did you get the test results?'

Maybe tonight's the night they tell me it's really over. Maybe I can ask them to put a bullet in my brain. If the test results were bad enough that would hardly be a crime. I would never dare to do it myself, that much I know.

'I met your daughter by the lift,' she says. 'She seemed upset.'

I swallow.

'It's not your job to discuss that with me. Send in the counsellor.'

I pause. Purse my lips.

'Or send the counsellor to my daughter,' I continue.

She looks at me with a frown. Disappointed. She is disappointed. Not in me as a patient, but as a mother.

'Nahid.'

I'm surprised that she knows my name. That she sees me as a person and not just a container of expanding cell masses and toxins.

'I understand that it's painful,' she says. 'I understand that it feels unfair. I understand that you are angry. I understand all that. And I have no say in the choices you make, or how you choose to live your life. My job is to fight the cancer. And to make sure that you are in as little pain as possible. That's all. So I will just say this: I recommend you try. I recommend you try to make your days feel meaningful. Spend time with your loved ones. Do fun things. As your doctor, I recommend it, Nahid, because then you'll have more energy. Do you understand? And that's all we want here. For you to have more strength. For longer.'

'Why do I need strength?' I reply. 'What will it lead to? I get a few more days, more days to be strong. Why can't it just end? Why do I have to continue? I'm going to die! Everyone knows that I'm going to die. Why should I continue?'

'Nahid,' Christina says. 'We're all going to die. I might die before you. Do you understand that? Your daughter could die at any time. In an accident, from some unknown condition. We don't know, we don't know anything. But if something happens to her, you'll be left with the memory of your last words to her. I'm just a doctor, but I can promise you that would be worse than cancer.'

You could call me an egoist. Some might say: You are selfish, Nahid. And I would hate anyone like that. I'd cry and I'd scream. I would say: What do you know? What do you know about what I've been through? What do you know about how lonely I've been? What do you know about how selfishly others have behaved towards me? I could say that, and the person would dislike me even more. They would say:

You feel sorry for yourself. You feel sorry for yourself, and that's egotistical, too. Why punish the innocent for wrongs committed against you? Don't you understand you're just passing down your pain. Don't you understand you're keeping the pain alive, ensuring that it survives you. Is that what you want? Do you want pain to be your legacy, pain to be your child's inheritance? I would look at this person, give them an angry look. My answer would be short.

Why should she be spared?

*

I wait until Christina leaves. Then I haul myself up and reach for my phone. *I'm coming*, I text. And then throw myself down on my back again.

'I'm doing this for Aram's sake,' I say aloud to myself.

But it's not true. I'm doing it for myself. The doctor is right. It hurts to hurt others. It hurts, because they turn their backs. That's the worst part. To be left alone. I don't want that. I want her to come back, want her to stand by my side. So I'll do what she wants this time. My phone beeps. *Good! I'll pick you up*, she texts. She's coming. That's all I need, and I let my eyes close. Sleep instead of fight. Rest and let the tumours take new breath inside my body.

In my stupor, I imagine it like a rape. I'm forced to experience my greatest fear: something unknown and unwanted penetrating my body and taking possession of it. Leaving a mess in its wake that can never be cleaned away. I think to myself, I've lost the fight for my own body. But perhaps the battle was already lost when I was born. Another girl, another disappointment.

Now we're together again in a car. She's holding my hand, and we're both looking out the window, out towards Strandvägen and the water. I had hoped it would be glittering, but it's not. It's dark and windy and foreboding.

'It's going to rain,' I say.

'It doesn't matter,' she replies.

The car pulls up in front of the Cirkus arena, and there are so many people that I have to catch my breath. It's been a long time since I saw so much life. She opens my door from outside, but I hesitate.

'I don't know if I can.'

She grabs my arm and pulls me out. Gently but with more force than I expected. I allow myself to be pulled, with shuffling feet. At some point we are joined by her friends. They look at me with eyes full of pity, and I look away. None of them know what to say to me. I sink into a soft chair. Just then the music starts, and it's as if I'm surrounded by a living presence, as if I'm wrapped in warmth and beauty and something as tender as a mother's hands. The music. The sound has something Persian in it, and she is like something from a fairy tale, the girl who steps out on stage. Laleh is her name. A spring tulip in an April storm. She starts to speak and her voice patters like gentle summer rain against my eardrums.

It takes me back to a time and place long since passed. Aram is still holding my hand, and for the first time I feel that it's OK. It's OK to die. I feel there is a warmth that awaits me. Papa's warmth. The warmth that once lived inside Masood. In Noora. I feel like Noora is waiting for me. I sink into the soft chair and feel my own smile. Feel myself press Aram's hand, tenderly like those mothering hands. She looks at me, and even in the darkness, I can see her surprise. My affection astonishes her.

I don't know if it was my warmth that did it or if Aram too was wrapped in that same sense of security by the darkness. By the girl on the stage. I hope I gave her something. Hope I helped her to grieve. But it was probably just the music. The poetry. She grew up on music and poetry, my daughter. Music and poetry is what gave her comfort, what gave her air to breathe, what nurtured her. But I was the one who gave her the music, and that makes me happy. At least I could give her music. Now the girl on the stage starts to sing. A child of war, like my daughter. Her words give Aram air. She sings of those who leave too soon and those who try to hold on, who won't let go. *Some die young*, she sings, and Aram lets out a cry. A quiet, quiet cry. She bows her head and starts to shake and I know she's weeping, my girl. My baby. She whimpers like a baby. She cries and trembles and whimpers like a baby and I know why. I know I'm the one who's going to die. That she's the one being left behind. I know I will abandon my child, and that she will lose her mother. I hold her hand more tightly and lean back in my chair. Rocking myself back and forth. That's just how it is. I will die and my child will lose her mother. For a moment, it feels good. It feels like that's how it was meant to be.

It's summer again. April's turned to May, May to June and once again they've raised the maypole on the lawn below. They're wearing their floral dresses and shouting their happy shouts. I hang out my window, as usual, with a cup of tea next to me. My mirror image demands attention, and I look at myself. Look properly. My hair is back. No chemotherapy for three months and the tumours have retreated. I'm cured! That's what I said to Christina on Monday, but she didn't agree.

'We'll see, Nahid,' she said.

I chose not to ask any more questions.

'Thank you,' I said instead, and she nodded at me.

Smiled gently.

'Have a lovely midsummer.'

'I will! I'm celebrating with my daughter and her boyfriend's family.'

I hesitated. But then I said, 'It's a tradition.'

I didn't tell her this was only the second time, because then we'd start talking about time again. Would this be the last time, and is it a tradition if it has only happened twice?

I've bought a new dress, a dress with big red flowers on it. It's hanging on the bathroom door and a pair of red sandals sit in the hall. I look forward to it. I want to ride in the car, out, out, over the water, bridges and islands.

Through all that beauty. I want to make good memories. So much beauty. Something lovely to keep inside me.

When I'm dressed, I stand in front of the mirror and pull out my lipstick. With slow and meticulous care, I paint my lips. Today nothing ends up outside the lines. Today I refuse to be the sick one. On this particular day, I'm not sick. On this day, all signs indicate I'll survive. It feels like I'm born again.

*

I immediately notice that something is different. They take the lift up together, then ring the doorbell. She's holding her car keys, clutching onto them. She keeps twisting and turning and rattling them, and I don't want to tell her to stop, because today I am not sick. But it's so annoying I finally shout.

'Stop that!'

She drops her keys in surprise, and he looks at me darkly. I turn my back on them and walk towards the lift. Hear they aren't following. They are still standing there whispering. He's comforting her. She's sick, I think. Today, I'm healthy, and she's ill. It's surely cancer, it would be. I've given her cancer. Today, I'm healthy, and she's dying. What if I am the one who gets to live, and she's the one who dies, leaving me behind. That thought scares me more than anything ever has.

In the car we all sit in silence. I, who had been looking forward to an easy day, to being happy. All of us. I try to read their backs. He seems fine. She's the one who is tense. I try to think of something to say. Something to ask. I realise I haven't needed to do that for a long time. She asks all the questions, and all I have to do is answer. It's hard to think of questions.

'How's work, Johan?' I hear myself say.

It wasn't the kind of question I had in mind, and it wasn't him I wanted to talk to.

He turns around. Looks happy.

'It's going well, Nahid. Thanks for asking. But it'll be nice to have some time off soon.'

He doesn't say any more, and I turn away and roll my eyes. All these empty words we say to each other. They don't mean anything at all.

'How do you feel? I heard it went well at the doctor's this week.'

I smile at him and make the victory sign. 'I won! The cancer is gone.'

She looks at me in the rearview mirror.

'The tumours are gone, I mean. I'm tumour free. So right now I don't have cancer, and that's something. Right, Johan?'

He reaches for my hand and squeezes it hard. 'It's a lot, Nahid.'

He has tears in his eyes, which I'm not prepared for. I'm not prepared for him to care, not in that way.

She clears her throat, looks at me in the rearview mirror again.

'We thought we'd stop at Delselius, Mama. Have a coffee and a vanilla bun. Is that OK with you?'

'Today? It's midsummer, are they open?'

'Yes, I called ahead and made sure,' she says.

I don't understand why it's so important, none of us are that crazy about pastries anyway. I say as much, and she smiles.

'No, I know. I just really want one. And it's been a long time, right? How long was it? Fifteen years ago?'

I nod, it was. Fifteen years ago we bought the apartment in the city and drove home to Gustavsberg in shock, sat in those very café chairs and ordered *semlor*, because it was February, and almost laughed out loud. I don't think any of us thought it would actually happen, but we managed it. Bought a new home, a different kind of home, and left everything else behind. Or so we thought, as everyone does when they flee, when they move. Now we're leaving it all behind. But that's not how it works. It comes with you, no matter how far you go. Still we celebrated moving on, and we were happy.

I want to say the words. It's been fifteen years since we had a happy moment together. But it sounded so incredibly sad in my own head, mostly because I wasn't sure we'd ever get another one again. You can't say it's been fifteen years since we were happy, until you're happy again. I wonder if maybe that's the hardest part. To be reminded of better times. Be reminded that it can be better. Be reminded that happiness is so close, that it's actually within reach.

'That's fine,' I say simply, and she looks relieved. As if she'd expected me to make a fuss.

*

We park near the square and climb out. It looks abandoned. Not just because it's midsummer, but because there's almost nothing left there. A pizzeria, a bakery, a video store, though there are hardly any video stores left anywhere else these days. The type of stores people actually go to wouldn't fit here. Rusta, Ica Maxi, McDonald's. Such places are built far from here, where there used to be forest. I wonder why they haven't torn down this old place. Done something else with it. I remember when we used to go here every day. Shop at Domus, pick up large packages from Iran at the post office, go to the movies at Folkets Hus. We discovered Sweden through this small square.

'It's a ghost town,' I say to her, and she takes my hand.

'I know. It's completely different now. But that doesn't matter, right? It doesn't affect us.'

I realise that I agree with her. This has nothing to do with us. We're not here any more, we left it behind us long ago.

Then I realise that she really means something else entirely. That this is too trivial to touch us. The loss of a place doesn't matter to those who have lost their people. Doesn't matter to those who are dying.

I lower my head. Say it still does. That I feel disturbed by it. A place you left, a place you've fled from, it shouldn't get to you, but it does anyway. All loss touches you. When death is near, you don't want to acknowledge that things can be lost.

We go into the Delselius Café, and everything looks like it used to. Glass dishes with traditional cakes and open sandwiches and cinnamon buns and vanilla buns. Blonde girls behind the counter, with the same striped aprons. Red velvet on the seats, the same fabric and the same chairs. It looks run down, not as nice and inviting as it felt back when Aram was small and we could only afford five-kronor buns and then only rarely.

Johan goes to the counter to order, and Aram leads me over to a big table by the window. We are the only customers inside. A couple of older men are drinking coffee on the terrace. Someone comes in to pick up a cake for their midsummer celebrations. It's a little dark inside, the sun is shining outside, and I still don't understand why we stopped here. She sits diagonally across from me and he takes the place next to her. On the tray lie a couple of buns and a Mazarin. The waitress brings us our coffee. I look at the clock on the wall, a big one like the clock that used to hang in Aram's classroom.

'Won't we be late to see your parents?'

'It's no problem.'

Johan glances at her. Aram gently shakes her head.

Leans forward and whispers in his ear.

He clears his throat.

'Nahid, there's something we want to tell you.'

'OK. Well, tell me then.' My heart is pounding, and I know it. This is about life and death. She is sick, she's the one who's dying now.

He looks at her again, and she looks away, so he clears his throat again.

'Well, Nahid, here's the thing, you . . . '

Aram rises abruptly from her chair, and he looks up in surprise. She looks like she wants to run away, and I feel the same. I don't want to be here. Why did they take me back here? To old memories and old disappointments just to add a new one.

He takes her hand and holds it tight. She remains standing there next to him.

'Nahid, you're going to be a grandmother.'

It goes black in front of my eyes. I think at first that I heard wrong. Or they're kidding, it's a joke to lighten the mood. I squint at him.

'What did you say?'

He becomes hesitant. Glances at her, but she looks away.

'Well, we're having a baby. You're going to be a grandmother.'

I grab the edge of the table, hard. 'Oh,' I moan. 'Oh, oh god.'

I'm trying to get up to go over to her, but I can't. My legs are trembling, and I feel like I might fall down. I want to say something. Something lighthearted. This day! So full of life. But I can't. Instead, I put my head in the crook of my arm and start to sob. Tears fall like a veil before my eyes, and I disappear into myself. Into my cancer, all my struggles. I think, this is everything I longed for. To receive some sign that I was not a redundant human being. I am more than a traitor. More than just the reason other people die and are unhappy. I think of my mother, sitting by the phone in her tiny apartment. I think about how she always expects the worst. About the way she sits there on the rug, guarding the front door and watching over the phone and sometimes she gets up and peers out between the curtains. I never called to have that conversation. I never called to say: Mama, I have cancer, and I'm going to die. And now I can call and tell her this instead: *Mama, we're going to have a baby!*

I look up at them. Aram has sat down on her chair again, and he holds her, his eyes red. She trembles in his arms.

'Is it true?' I ask. 'Is it for real?'

She doesn't look up. She cries into his chest. But he nods, nods and smiles.

I wipe my face with a napkin, but can't stop. Can't stop. I, who was supposed to die. I, who should die and go to waste. Now I have this to live for.

'Thank you,' I say. 'Thank you.'

She won't meet my eyes, but I don't mention that. I stand up and go to her and throw my arms around her, and she lowers her shoulders. I feel her relax against me, and I push my wet cheek against hers and say thank you once more. I say, I'm here for you. I'll be here for you. She starts to cry again, and he throws his arms around us both, and we sit there like a heap, as a human heap. Another type of meat mountain. She, I, he and the little one growing inside her.

The little one. That's all I want. If I get this, I won't ask for anything more.

'I will be the world's best grandma.'

She looks up at me, looks straight at me. Her eyes are full of doubt. Doubt and the other thing that never disappears, the splinter, the gleam, the naive childishness. Her hope.

Her hope in me.

*

We drive on, down that road I've travelled so many times before. We pass forests and beaches. We drive over Djurö Bridge and the water glitters so it flickers in my head. What a beautiful place and today I am a part of it. A part of life and beauty. Today I will not die. Today I'm a grandmother. Today I am immortal in every way you can be immortal. It tingles in my stomach. I fought cancer, and this is my reward.

I think of the big trees out on the island. I think, my grandchild will not be like me. She will be a child of roots, not sand. She will live where she was born. Her roots will penetrate deep into the earth. I created that. I was the one who made sure my grandchild could have both freedom and roots. My escape made that possible. I clasp my hands in my lap. Let the air out between my lips and sit up a little straighter. Aram looks at me through the rearview mirror again. Our eyes meet, and I see her smile.

His parents don't know about the pregnancy, and we tell them together. I am one of the ones who tell them, and it feels good. This is my grandchild. They already have four.

'Oh, how lovely,' says his mother. That's all. It must be the difference between knowing death and never having faced it. Life's greatness passes you by.

We sit at the lunch table and pour wine into glasses, and I ask them to fill up mine. We toast and I take a big gulp. We all laugh, me the loudest. But soon, I want to go, go to the beach and the woods and be alone with my thoughts. I say I'm going to rest, and everyone understands. I take off my shoes and leave them on the jetty. I want to feel the stones and sand under my feet. I walk down to the beach and sit with my arms around my legs. There is a slide here. I didn't notice it last year. There's a basket of plastic toys under the dock. A truck peeks out over the edge. I want to buy a bucket and spade, I think. A little bucket and spade for her, because I know it's a girl. A girl to take Noora's place. A girl to fill the void.

It's when I'm helping to clear the table that I notice. I walk down the path, between the towering trees, with a tray in hand. Making an effort to be healthy and capable. So I don't have to say I can't, so I don't drop everything and smash the wine glasses against the stone. I focus my gaze on the tray, but still from the corner of my eye I see that something is wrong. I look again. The roots are gone. I turn around, look at the other side. They are gone, completely gone. Small splinters on the ground testify to the fact that they were there, but they've been pulled out. I put down the tray, get down on my knees and feel the ground. Just earth. I hear footsteps behind me, Johan's mother calling to me. Asking if everything is OK.

'They're gone, the roots. The ones that used to lie here?' It's a question, because I think she may have moved them in some way. They may still exist, just not here.

'Yes, that's right, isn't it nice,' she replies. 'We cleared them away this spring. So much work, they're more stubborn than you'd think. But didn't it turn out nice?'

I must have looked at her blankly because she stops.

'And we wouldn't want the grandkids tripping on them.'

I don't know what to say to her, and she probably thinks my silence has to do with my health anyway. Thinks I'm sitting on the ground because I'm sick.

'Leave the tray, and I'll ask Nils to get it,' she says and walks past me towards the house.

I follow her with my eyes until the red door slams shut behind her. Then I dig my fingers into the earth, digging as deep as I can go. They have to be there still, somewhere below the surface. Surely roots can't just be pulled out, can't disappear. But my fingers never reach them.

Watching Aram's belly grow is the most beautiful sight I've seen in my life. I ask her to sit next to me on the sofa so that I can touch it. Sometimes I go over to her while she's making tea or doing the dishes and lift up her shirt. Put my cold hands on her skin. It makes her uncomfortable, I can see that in her eyes. Her watchful gaze. I understand. She wants to protect her child. She wants to protect her child from me.

I think it's good she wants to be a protector, because it's difficult. It's difficult to do and sometimes it's difficult to want to do. Sometimes you feel you need protecting. Like even your own child can handle more than you. I wish it wasn't so. That I came from something else, that I could handle things better on my own. But that's not how it is.

I sneak a glance at her, stare at her when she doesn't notice. Trying to make out if she's damaged. Damaged like me. So damaged that she'll forget to do any protecting, that she'll choose to avoid it. I want to ask her what she thinks about all this. If she thinks she'll end up like me. But how can I ask that without starting a conversation I absolutely don't want to have? No, I'm not going to talk to her about the past. I've decided that. Sometimes I've noticed she wants to. She tries to bring it up. Wants me to explain. Maybe ask forgiveness. But then I say something that gives her second thoughts.

Something that tells her I won't talk, that I'm not a person to seek comfort from. I never have been, and I won't spend my last months consoling her. I'm the one going through treatments and nausea and shortness of breath, lying like a vegetable waiting for death to pluck me and carry me away. So instead I call her one day. She's at work and doesn't have time, but I say it's important, so she goes out onto the street to listen to me.

'Can you be a good mother?' I ask.

She falls silent.

'Will you be a good mother?'

'I don't understand,' she replies. 'What do you mean?'

'I'm not sure you can! You're not strong enough for a birth. And taking care of a child is difficult. Can you handle it?'

She inhales sharply, it's as if I can hear every molecule bouncing against her throat and down into her body. Then she exhales. Heavily.

'Mama. I'm hanging up now. Please, don't call back, don't call me again today.' She hangs up. In my ear. Before I have time to say anything else. I stare at the phone in my hand while my throat thickens and my chest swells, almost bursts. I hate her! She makes me feel alone. Abandoned and unimportant. In that moment, I hate her.

I text: *How could you do that to me. I'm sick!*

There is no answer.

I ring her doorbell. It's Saturday morning, and she doesn't know I'm coming. I don't know what she will say, but I had to come. I couldn't call her and risk her not picking up.

It takes a while for anyone to open the door. At first, it's completely quiet so I press the bell again. Then I hear a body moving, slowly. I'm not sure she's headed for the door so I ring again. Only after I press the button, do I remember that this is the way she was informed after Masood's death. Police officers rang at her door, again and again, when she didn't open up right away. I think it's the same thing again, this is her lot in life. Death knocking on her door. As it was ours to watch Rozbeh fall to the ground and bleed away from us. As it was our lot that Noora never came home. I think how her life must be a repetition of mine, that's the only possibility. The only justice. So I press the doorbell again.

When she opens the door I can see she is miserable. 'Mama. What is it?'

She has a hard time even forcing the words out, and her movements reveal she's in pain.

I step forward and put my hand on her arm. 'What is it, honey? What's going on?'

'I don't know, Mama.' She leans against the wall and hunches over. 'Something is wrong.'

She lifts her hand to her belly, and I drop my handbag on the floor. We both flinch from the bang.

'No, no,' I cry. 'No, this can't happen.'

'Mama, please. Sit down, please. I'll call Johan.'

'I'll call an ambulance,' I say. 'I'm calling an ambulance!'

This can't happen. This was not what I meant, this isn't our lot. Her lot. Our lot. We need this child. We deserve this child. This child is our consolation. I sink down onto the chair in the hall, panting heavily, trying to catch my breath. I hear her talking on the phone, softly. And then again, in a more authoritative tone. She'll fix this, I think, she can fix it.

'Mama, do you want to come with me?'

'Where are we going?'

'To the hospital.'

Then she looks at me one more time. With doubt. 'Are you up to it, Mama?'

I don't know. I don't know if I'm up to it.

'Not if something goes wrong.'

She laughs. It's a harsh laugh. 'Then it's best you don't come.'

She's dressed now, and the front door is open.

'I have to go.' She doesn't look at me. Walks out.

Closes the door.

I'm sitting there, staring at my trembling hands. Thinking how it's all going to hell again. I wish we'd been allowed to be happy a little longer. I wish there'd been more joy. I wonder if my memories of that midsummer's day will still feel beautiful the next time we cross that bridge. Or if beautiful moments only count if nothing changes. If the beauty is allowed to remain, undisturbed.

I hear a car drive up, and I think of her standing down there on the street. I think how all this ugliness hasn't made her stop trying. I jump up and rush towards the taxi. It's about to pull away when I jerk open the door and climb in. She looks up from her phone, surprised.

'I'm here,' I say.

She nods, turns away. After a moment, she reaches for my hand. We hold hands the rest of the way. It's quiet in the car and I think, here we are again. She and I, in a car, trying to create something beautiful.

*

When we arrive, they see us immediately. I'd been prepared to shout and argue, but it's not needed. They take babies seriously, I think. New life is more important than a life that is almost over.

She asks me to wait in the waiting room. I don't understand, and I protest, but her face silences me. She doesn't trust me, and that's that. She walks into a room with a nurse, and everything is still. For a long time everything is still. I'm sitting with my handbag in my lap, hugging it. Wondering where Johan is, but I'm glad we're alone. That it's me who's here, it's me who's helping. Or at least I should be helping! I shouldn't be sitting here powerless.

'Excuse me,' I say to a passerby. 'Is there a cafeteria here?'

'Follow me,' the person says, and takes me to a shop.

I'm relieved, in some indescribable way. As if the store allows me to be who I want to be. Someone who does something. A helper. I find a basket and start gathering stuff. Carrot juice, to give her strength. I take two. A small bag of crisps. I pause by the magazines, but I don't know what she reads. I try to remember. Wish I knew, because she would know. She would know what I want. I decide in the end to not buy any at all. That's better than seeing her disappointed.

Now I don't know what to do. I look towards the flower buckets and remember that day in the hospital, when I asked her to take the ugly bouquet with her. I turn away. And then

I see it, the stand with small teddy bears and giraffes and baby blankets and other things designed for when there's a happy outcome. I stretch out my hand and touch a mouse, a blue mouse of soft, smooth fabric that is wrapped in a small blanket. I lift it up and my eyes fill with tears, and I want to give up. I want to go up to the cancer ward and ask for a room and say, I'm here to die. But I put the mouse in the basket and take it to the checkout. I ride the lift up to the maternity ward. I act the way I should, for once.

When I arrive, a nurse approaches me. I swallow hard. I think now's the time. Now I have to prove I'm a mother, I'm a nurse. I have to prove who I am. But I just stand there.

'Your daughter would like to see you.'

I nod. 'How ... what? Do you know anything?'

I don't think she hears me. Or maybe she doesn't want to answer. I squeeze the mouse in my pocket. I couldn't put it in the bag, couldn't hand it over, just in case. In case.

The nurse goes in front of me, knocks gently on the door before opening it. I struggle to hold down the lump in my throat, not to let it burst. Inside Aram is sitting, reclining in a hospital bed. Her stomach is bare and there are small electrodes attached to it. She's turned away so I turn too. Trying to suppress my panic.

'Mama,' she says softly. Her tone surprises me. I don't know if I've heard it before. It's her mother voice, I think. She sounds like that because she's a mother.

'Mama, look.' She reaches for me, and I go to her. I don't want to look at the wires and machines, so I look at her face and see she's happy. I want to start breathing again, but I don't dare.

'Do you hear it, Mama?' I don't understand what she means, but when I listen I hear a quick, rhythmic sound: Thump, thump, thump.

'It's a pulse. A heart. Look there.'

I look at the monitor and see. Heartbeats. Tiny rapid heartbeats. I don't think I understand at first. I just look.

'There she is,' says Aram. 'She's doing well.'

Something bursts in my stomach and rushes up through my throat. I take hold of the bed. Trying to see through the tears.

'There she is. She's doing well,' I repeat. 'She's doing well.'

I crawl up on the bed, and we lie next to each other, watching. The waves flow by on the screen. We lie there a long time, waiting for the test results, waiting to go home again. I don't think about waiting. I don't think about anything. I just watch and listen.

It's only when we pull our coats on that I remember why I rang at her door. The cancer. It's back. Metastases everywhere. In my stomach and lungs and liver.

I glance at her. She looks so relieved. So fulfilled. She's not thinking about how weak my steps seem, so I decide to give her this day. This day belongs to life.

I have made a nest on the sofa with pillows and blankets. I even managed to make tea. All by myself. No one knows I've started treatment again. I never thought I'd be able to keep such a thing to myself. But it scared me, what happened that day we went to the hospital. That tiny life waiting in her belly. I have to protect her. If I've ever protected anything in my life, it will be that baby.

When Aram was born, I thought she would be the one who replaced Noora. That she came instead of Noora. I thought she would be safe, that no one would hurt her. But it was too early. We were still in the middle of the nightmare. The pain and grief couldn't be prevented. She became part of what was going on. Persecution, war, our escape. But now. Here's a life that can be free from evil. A life that will replace mine, replace Noora's, will even replace Aram's. This is our chance, and I'm not going to spoil it for anything. I go to my treatments, and I vomit quietly. It won't be possible to keep it secret for ever, but as long as it works, as long as I can, I'll protect her.

I pull the blanket over my legs and grab the landline. My mother's number is on speed dial. I'm going to call and tell her a little girl is coming to Earth. A girl who belongs to us. We'll be four generations of women on earth at the same time. I think, this is my way of paying her back for what I took from her.

It takes a while for someone to answer. I wait. I suppose she needs time to move in that small apartment, I won't hang up and make her disappointed she didn't get there in time. Finally, after perhaps twenty rings, I hear a strange voice. It's the neighbour. We exchange a few pleasantries before I finally ask if Mama is home.

'*Ey vay*, has no one told you. *Khanom* was taken by ambulance to the hospital!'

'Why?'

I hear my voice harden, and even though it's not this woman's fault, it feels that way. We're going to be four generations on this earth! She's getting a new Noora, I'll give her a new Noora!

'It's best that you call there,' the neighbour says and gives me a number. I write it down in silence. Hang up without saying thank you.

I start calling my sisters, but no answer. I try over and over, calling every single one. Finally, Maryam picks up.

'Maryam, what's going on?'

'*Aziz*, nothing,' she says. Then she's quiet.

'I know Mama is in hospital. I know nobody is answering my calls. So something's going on, tell me!'

'You don't need to worry about it,' she says. 'Focus on getting well! We'll take care of all this.'

No, no. Not now, please, not now. I lift a pillow and scream into it.

'Maryam, I want to talk to my mother. I need to talk to my mother. Where is she?'

I hear her whispering, talking to someone else. I hear that they are trying to work out how to deal with me, what to say.

'Maryam,' I cry. 'Where is my mother?'

'Please calm down. There there.' She pauses. 'Mama had a stroke. She's ... unconscious. We don't know if she's going to wake up again.'

'Yes, yes, she will wake up! You have to wake her, Maryam. I have news. Aram's baby is a girl. I have to tell her.'

She's silent, my strong sister. I hear her trying to regulate her breathing, trying to stay calm. She is still trying to protect me, even though she's never succeeded. None of them ever managed that, and now Mama is dying, and no one is helping me. They have to help me wake her up!

'Maryam, you have to make her wake up. Do you hear me? I need to talk to her. I need it, Maryam, you don't understand.'

'I'll call you later, *aziz*,' she says, and hangs up. And that's all.

I sink into the couch, among my pillows, curl into a foetal position and whimper.

'Mama, Mama ...'

I try to rock myself into some kind of peace. My gaze settles on the puke bucket next to the sofa. The half-drunk meal replacements lying on the rug. I'm alone. I'm so piercingly alone. Loneliness lies heavy over my body. My entire body feels its weight. I try to lift my arm to wipe the wetness from my cheeks, but it hangs limp at my side. I can't move it. Suddenly, the room spins and flickers before my eyes. It's like a carousel spinning faster, faster. I want to get off! I want to get off, but I get nowhere.

The evening Masood came home and told me Saber was dead was the night hope died. The hope of a new start. When Masood lifted up my daughter, my very being, in his arms and started to beat me. The hope of making anything other than pain from the pain died. We couldn't stay. We couldn't protect ourselves, and we couldn't protect our child.

When he was done he backed away with Aram still in his arms. She screamed so loud I thought, now they'll come, any moment they'll come. There could only be criminals in a home where the baby screams like that. The kind who must be executed. He backed off until he hit the wall, and then he sank down. I thought he was going to drop her, because everything was happening with such force, but he didn't. He held tight. It calmed me. In some strange way, I became calm in the chaos. I thought, he has her. He won't hit her or kick her. Even if I never manage to crawl up from this rug, he has her. He won't let her go. At that moment that was all I cared about.

He kicked me just like Maryam was kicked that first time. I thought about that as I lay there. Now it's happening again, the same thing's happening again. And when the same thing repeats itself, you think it's meant to be. This is the way it was always meant to be.

We froze in that position. Him against the wall. Aram in his arms with her head turned in to his armpit and her little rump in my direction. And me, there on the rug. My cheek against the roughness. My eyelashes against my cheekbones. I think it was the shock that overtook us. I want to believe that. That shock turned us into people who beat each other. Into different people who never found a way back to who we really were. Or to who we could have been. We froze like that, and it was a long time until we moved. Aram fell silent finally. Fell asleep. I know I thought: We've chosen the wrong path. I know I thought that already then. We couldn't afford to stay here, motionless. We had to go. We had to warn the others. We had to find a new hiding place.

*

We woke near dawn. Aram whimpered, and it made our bodies react. We didn't look at each other. I think we were ashamed, that we both felt ashamed. Back then I still thought I had some reason for shame. Because I was the kind of woman who was beaten by her husband. I felt shame for who I was and shame for whom I'd chosen. We got up off the floor without a word, and started to gather our belongings. There wasn't much. Some clothes. A couple of blankets. A few pieces of our wedding china. We'd left most of it with Masood's father. Just for a while, we thought. Just until this blows over. Until everything calms down again. But we understood that morning, as we gathered the fragments of our life and threw them into our small suitcases, that it wasn't going to happen. It wouldn't be over, it would never calm down. Our things, possessions that together could have built a home, a life, they'd be left behind in someone else's storage. Soon enough someone would go in there, think maybe I'll borrow this bureau or this dress for my newborn daughter. The dresses I knitted or sewed on my mother's sewing machine, every one made by me.

When we finished, I tied a wrap around my upper body, and Masood placed Aram inside it. She was silent, dead silent. As if she knew it, knew everything. And so we went down the stairs. A boy with a rug over his shoulder and two small suitcases in his hands. A girl with a baby against her body. We opened the door carefully and Masood stuck his head out, waved at me when he saw that the street was empty. And so we walked off into the dim morning light. We didn't know where we were going, we were just trying to get as far away as possible. Masood cried silently. I knew he wept for Saber. I hoped he was also crying for me. For what he'd done to me. But I don't think so. I don't think he even remembered. I think he forgot about it every time, as soon as it was over. He repressed it immediately.

*

We stood in the middle of the city, at Imam Hussein Square. That's not what it used to be called. It used to be called something else. Something without the word Imam in it, but I don't remember what. Masood stood inside a telephone booth and tried to find a new place for us. I looked at the crowd moving around us frantically, almost in panic, even though the sun had barely had time to rise. Looked at the smouldering wake of the latest air raid. At the soldiers marching in my direction and beyond. I pressed Aram against my pounding heart and felt my own pulse in her body. *This is no place for a child*, I thought. *We have to get out of here.*

'I've arranged us somewhere new,' Masood said and lifted our suitcases again.

I didn't move, and he looked questioningly at me. 'Masood, we have to get out of here.'

'We are on the way, come!' But I stood there.

'No, I don't mean that. I mean, we have to go. Flee. We have to leave Iran, Masood.'

Just then Aram gurgled, laughed with a toothless smile.

We both turned our eyes towards her. Stared at the pure joy of living streaming out of her. Then we laughed too, first him and then me. We stood there in the middle of our fear and laughed, and he put his arm around me and pressed me to him. Now I realise I should have been uneasy, fearful. Faced with this man who had beaten me bloody and blue while holding my child in his arms. But I wasn't. I leaned against him, seeking shelter. He was the safest place in my life. It took a long time for anything to feel safer than him.

*

A few weeks later, Masood came home with a brown envelope under his arm. His sweater was drenched with sweat, his hands trembling. I sat on the floor with Aram in a new windowless room. She crawled around me in circles on the rug that comprised our home, and I didn't understand how she managed it. I didn't understand how she could thrive there. With no light or air. That she was able to find any energy to move in that vacuum surprised me.

He opened the envelope and emptied its contents for me. Three small things. Paper and ink. On the surface, not much. But I gasped.

'Masood,' I said hesitantly. 'Masood!'

He sank down, lay down on his side with his head in my lap. His body was still shaking, and now I understood that it was from adrenaline. Fear and adrenaline. He buried his head in my skirt and I stroked his hair while I stared at the three small booklets. What if they weren't good enough. What if something went wrong. What if we used them, and it all still went to hell.

I lifted one up, the top one. It felt authentic, the weight felt right in my hand. I opened it and flipped through. There was a photo of me, and the name Noora Pooreh. A false name. I closed my eyes tightly. It was happening now, it was really happening. We were going to flee, and this was who I was, who I would be. A false person and my Noora constantly with me, like a shadow.

I opened the other passports and looked at the pictures. Masood, with wide eyes and terror in his gaze. And then her. My little baby. One year old and a babbling smile. I wondered how a small child flees. Why would any baby need to flee. I wondered what would come to mind when she thought of this country. Her country that she would never know. I wondered what would become of her. I wondered that most, what would become of her. Setareh, it said. He had chosen the names, and I thought it was a good choice. The star that would lead us through the night.

'This is for her sake, right?'

Masood looked up at me.

'I hope so,' he replied, and at that moment I felt like we were children too. Twenty-four-year-old, wasted children. We had no idea what we were doing. We kept telling ourselves we had a responsibility, we needed to escape for her. She shouldn't lose her parents, her life. She deserved a future. That's why we were leaving the fight. That's why we were leaving our families, our country. That's why we had to abandon and betray them. But I don't know. I don't think it was true. I think we did it for our own sake. For our own selfish reasons. Because we didn't want to end up like Noora and Rozbeh and Saber.

Because we didn't want to die.

*

Fake passports were expensive and so were airport smugglers. We didn't pay. Masood didn't want to tell me at first where the money came from. He didn't want to involve any more people than necessary. Get anyone in deeper than they already were. Later I understood that his uncle paid. That we owed him our freedom.

Masood didn't want me to tell my mother.

'For her own sake,' he said, but then he changed his mind. 'For our sake. You know how she can be. If she starts to scream and cry . . . It will attract attention and she could end up in interrogation and who knows.'

'Should I leave my country without saying goodbye to my mother, Masood? Is that what you want me to do?'

We sat on the rug in our tiny room whispering. So afraid were we of persecution. We didn't know where they were, how they listened. We didn't know if they knew about us, or how much they knew.

But Saber, he knew everything. He was the only one in our group who'd had information about all of us. We put on blindfolds before we went into a meeting, so we didn't know what the others looked like. So we wouldn't be able to identify each other. We'd heard stories about what happened when you were arrested. They sat you in a car and drove you around the city and told you to point out familiar faces. Whoever was participating in meetings. Whoever you knew from underground. Whoever was handing out flyers at night. People like us. And that was just the beginning. Then came the torture, rape, threats of execution, all for more information. More names. We had to be strangers to each other.

Saber, he knew everything. Our grief when the news came was mixed with fear for our own lives. What had they done to him before they killed him? How faithful had he been to us in those agonising final hours? Some part of me wanted to believe he'd betrayed us. Then I wouldn't be the only traitor.

It took a few months for everything to be ready. We kept our suitcases packed and moved like nomads around the city. The rumours reached us, how they'd arrested more and more of our comrades. We all moved around, but we left traces behind us. It was impossible not to.

Masood repeated again and again that it wasn't Saber's fault so many were being arrested. It couldn't be Saber who had named names. He would never do that.

'They killed him because he was silent!'

He said this as if he were trying to convince himself, and I didn't say otherwise. I didn't know. I just rocked Aram in my arms, sang old songs and whispered: 'It's OK, everything's OK.' I tried to convince myself. The truth is that I was scared to death, and not only was I afraid of dying, but I was full of shame. Shame that we were leaving the chaos we helped create. Shame for Rozbeh and his parents. Shame for my lack of principles, shame I hadn't dared to stand up for anything at all during that interrogation. A profound shame that I would leave my mother with the loss of two daughters, a war and a revolution that had taken her country from her. I was ashamed, and in my shame, I told myself, this is for Aram. *This is for Aram.* Many of us said that later, much later, when things got difficult in a different way, when we couldn't understand the language, and people called us towel heads, and we wondered how anyone could survive that cold. *This is for the children.* But our heroism was not that great.

*

Only Masood's father knew that we were leaving. His father and his uncle who'd paid. I couldn't let it go, of course.

'Why can't my mother know if your father does?' He looked at me with tired eyes.

'Please,' he replied. 'Don't make this any harder than it needs to be. It's already hard. It's already so hard.'

I thought I'd tell her anyway. I would sneak off. Go to her, hold her for a long time, tell her everything. Tell her it would all be OK. That this wasn't a loss, but a win. A win for Aram, a win for us.

'We're leaving so you won't lose us,' I was going to say. And she would understand. She would hug me back, tight. She would forgive me for Noora, and she would thank me for taking care of everything, so she didn't have to worry any more.

But I knew it wouldn't be like that. I knew she would throw herself on the ground and hit herself in the face and scream at God and his fundamentalists, screaming *stop taking my children away from me.* She would scream and hit and the neighbours would come out and ask questions, and she'd yell out the answer and someone in the crowd would look at me in a different way than the others and that person would sneak off and pick up the phone and make a call and before I'd managed to lift my mother from the ground again, a van would have stopped in front of the house and guards would have jumped out and then I'd be gone. I knew Masood was right. But all my anger, all my sorrow, was directed at him. We had taken Noora from my mother, and now he was taking my mother away from me. I could never forgive him for that.

We were in the refugee camp by the time I finally got hold of a phone and found a way to use it. It had been several weeks since we left, several weeks since she'd heard from me.

The camp was comprised of small summer cottages in a forest, outside a small town that we never went back to. It was beautiful. Even amidst my worry I could see that. The forest was beautiful. This place was beautiful. I used to sit on a bench with Aram in my lap and tell her to look. Look at the tall pine trees, at the moss and the inviting boulders. I pointed to the birds chirping and the dogs that passed by on a lead. I put her in the swing and gave her a push and she almost reached the green branches hanging down from the sky. She gurgled and laughed and started to walk and run in those woods. There was air and light, and I thought it's obvious. It's obvious this is better. I said it out loud to myself, but I couldn't quite believe it.

In the reception there was a phone with a timer on it, and you had to pay for the call afterwards. It cost so much to call Iran at the time, and we had so little money. Masood sat next to me and said I should keep it short and I looked at him and wondered how you were supposed to do that. How were you supposed to tell your mother you've fled to another continent, that you might never see her again. I wondered how you kept something like that short.

It took a couple of tries before the call went through. When I think about it today, how hard we struggled to get in touch. It really felt like we had lost them for ever, our families. But finally it worked, and I pulled so hard on the telephone cord while I was waiting to hear my mother's voice that the receptionist put her hand on mine and squeezed it.

'*Hello!*'

She sounded upset, and I looked anxiously at Masood. Thought it might be easier to hang up, it might be easier to never have this conversation. To never have had it.

'*Maman.*' My voice was trembling, and I decided to let it. Let it gush out of me. '*Mamaaan.*'

I heard her crying, heard her sob and minutes passed while we cried together over the phone. I know Masood had his eye on the timer, and I thought perhaps this is the way to do it, just like this. You weep together over the phone. Maybe that's what you do, every time you hear the other voice on the phone. That was all we did for years.

When I looked at the timer, it was up to three minutes and twenty-six seconds, and we hadn't said a word. My eyes met Masood's, and his face was apologetic, but he put his finger down on the hook. The sound of my mother disappeared.

'It's OK. She already knows everything, you know that.'

I wanted to tell him it wasn't enough that his father had told her, that she had all the information. I wanted to explain. I wanted to talk about it. But I couldn't get anything out. I took the phone in my arms and hugged it tightly. Wept and hugged.

Masood stood next to me, bewildered. There are things you can't understand in advance. How utterly difficult it is to be a part of someone else's grief when you yourself are aching so much. He walked away eventually and the receptionist took over. She wasn't a receptionist really, but somebody who was hired to manage us. Manage our wounded souls. She stood beside me for a while, but even she didn't know what to do. What you are supposed to do. So she embraced me. I disappeared into her big, motherly arms and she pressed me to her, and she cried too. Her body, her upper arms quivered as she rocked me back and forth. It made me sob even harder. The feeling of being enveloped in someone else: in an unfamiliar body when you've lost the bodies that used to envelop you.

Sonja was her name. There were many tears at our refugee centre, and Sonja cried with us all. She gave us a lot of comfort. I wish I could find her, I wish there was a Sonja for me now.

Mama never forgave me for leaving her. I hoped one day she would. Understand more good came from our escape than bad. She never accepted it. She thought we could have stopped doing whatever we were up to and just hidden. Hidden ourselves away from politics and revolution. Found a village far out in the countryside and stayed there until everything blew over. And the war, the war ended a few years after we left. We could have hidden from the war. We could have hidden Masood so he didn't have to fight. Or at least we could have come back when the war was over.

'Even if that'd worked, Mama, even if everything you say worked, we don't want to live under an Islamic dictatorship,' I said to her once, over the phone. Then the line was cut. I heard a distinct drone, like the sound the TV used to make when programming ended for the evening. And then silence. When I tried to call back, I reached an automated voice telling me the number was no longer in service. It was only temporary, but at that moment I thought they'd taken her away from me again.

We could hear that they were listening. The click when someone picked up the phone. The noise. Sometimes voices. Sometimes they came and went. Click click click click. I had to resist the impulse to shout at them, scream at them to leave us alone. We had fled. We weren't there. We had nothing to do with them. But I didn't dare. My mother still lived there, and I couldn't cause her any more trouble. I'd done enough, more than anyone should ever have to endure.

*

And when I finally call with the news, the good news, they say I can't talk to her. Say she can't talk. She's lying unconscious in a hospital bed, and I may never talk to her again. *I have to tell you*, I think as I lie there unconscious in my darkness. The words echo inside me.

I have to tell you. I have to tell you.

*

I know where I am even though I can't open my eyes. I recognise the smell. Antiseptic and revolting at the same time. Open wounds and infected lungs and decaying bodies. I try to move my lips, try to protest. Say I want to go home. But they are dry, dried shut. And I can't control them.

Aram takes my hand. She must have stood over me, waiting for the slightest movement.

'Mama. Mama, I'm here.'

I stop trying. Let my eyelids rest. I disappear again.

Next time I wake up my eyelids open by themselves. The room is dark. Empty. I'm plugged into a machine, and it sounds like it should. Regular beeps. I let out a huge breath.

'I'm alive. I'm alive.'

I mutter it as I look for the red button. I push hard, for a long time. Even though I know that doesn't make any difference. They hear the same signal no matter how hard I push. But I'm pushing it for dear life.

'I'm alive!' I burst out when the nurse comes into the room. She's round and old and nice and she laughs.

'What luck!'

She comes over and takes my hand.

'I'm glad you're awake, Nahid. Your daughter's been here every day waiting for you.'

I press her hand hard, so hard it must hurt. 'What happened? What happened to me?'

'You had a stroke, Nahid.'

A stroke. Like my mother.

'That can happen, you know. From the tumours.'

I know. I know that. But I don't want to. I don't want to have a stroke. I don't want to have tumours.

'I need to talk to my mother.'

The nurse nods and fiddles with the tubes on my arm. 'Yes, there there. Soon, the night will pass.'

I understand that she doesn't take me seriously. That she thinks I'm delirious. I know that's what people do when they're about to die. The elderly people I cared for always called out for their mothers. Sometimes I'd sit on a chair in the hallway and listen. A symphony of agony. The last moment of life. Everyone cries for their mothers. 'I'm awake. I know what I'm saying. Please. Give me my phone. I have to call my mother.'

She pats my head. 'It's the middle of the night, dearie.'

'You don't understand, I need my mother. This is an emergency!'

'There, there,' she says as she picks up her things.

And then she goes.

I raise the red button and press hard again. But I already know that she's not coming back, that she sees me as I saw my old-timers. Tears wet my pillow and I shake my head with what little movements I'm able to produce. I'm not old! All the weak bodies I've helped in their last hour. They were ninety, even a hundred years old. Why didn't I get more. Why did I get so little.

I'm going to die, I think. I'm really going to die.

'Why didn't you tell me, Mama? Why didn't you say anything?'

Aram is sitting next to me, stroking my hair.

'I wanted to take care of it,' I say to her. 'I wanted to take care of it myself.'

'You don't need to do that, Mama. I'm here.'

I want to tell her I was trying to protect her, but I don't know if that's true. I was trying to protect the baby. My grandchild. I wanted to protect my own immortality. Myself.

'It will go away again,' I say. 'It disappeared the last time. It will disappear again.'

She is leaning back, with her hand on her belly. It's huge. I tell her that, and she laughs. So soft again. I see in her eyes that she is happy. She has a kind of bubble around her, and in it I have no place. She has a bubble of gentleness and serenity and happiness that is for her child. I'm something she handles. Handles in order to get back to her own world. I think: she won't miss me when I die. She'll have something new, something much better than me. That child is going to take my place in her life, and she will think it's a good exchange. She'll come to feel that the price for my child was my mother dying, and it was worth it. That's what she'll think. Maybe say it to someone, someday. I think: maybe it wasn't good after all. The child coming. I think: the child will make me die alone. I'll die even lonelier.

I call my sisters every day. They tell me about our mother, but I don't know if they're telling the truth. They say she's still in the hospital. She is conscious now. But she only receives visitors a few minutes a day. And she doesn't have access to a telephone.

'But can you tell her, Maryam? Can you say that Aram is going to have a little daughter?'

'We don't want to make her too emotional. The doctors say that's bad for her. You know that, right, Nahid? It's not good for her?'

I want to scream at them, but I keep it inside. I'm proud of that, I manage to hold back. They're keeping my mother away from me, but I think that's what I deserve. I was the one who left her and them. My rights have long since been exhausted. So I keep calling several times a day. Trying to make out from their tone of voice if something has happened. But I also know that she might as well be dead. My mother may already be gone. They wouldn't tell me, not now. What difference would it make? If they wait long enough, they'll never have to tell me.

Christina wants to stop the chemo again. The stroke scared her. They think I'm weak. That treatment will kill me. They're hoping they can radiate away whatever is big enough, whatever they can get to. But we all know that won't save me.

Aram has hope for radiation. She believes in it.

'You have to do it, Mama. You have to do everything you can,' Aram said after our conversation with the doctor.

'If radiation could have killed it, they'd have used it from the start. It doesn't matter.'

'You can't give up. Mama. Do you hear me? You can't give up. You have to let them try radiation. You can't stop now. Not now.'

I wonder if she really wants me here. Or if she's just saying that. Just saying what you are supposed to say.

I often think about when we fled. Wonder if what we did was right. Right and wrong, it's so hard to know which is which as the years go by and everything gets complicated, knotted. Sometimes I wonder if right and wrong are even the opposite of each other, or just two ways of expressing the same thing.

If you think in terms of life and death, then fleeing was the right choice. It should be that simple. We fled political persecution and a war. The best chance for our survival was escape. And we survived. We did. For thirty years we survived.

But every sibling and cousin we have, Masood and I, who stayed is still alive. Everyone, that is, who was alive when we fled. Those who hadn't yet died in 1984, they are still alive. While Masood is dead. And I'm dying.

Why did Masood's heart stop? Why did cancer attack my body? One wonders. But at the same time, how could our hearts beat so long? How could our bodies take everything that's happened since the day we got on the plane with those false passports?

I watch the news. So many refugees streaming across the sea. The world has changed. When we fled our biggest problem was how to get out of our own country. Once we figured that out, we bought a plane ticket. Flew to freedom. These people. They fight their way here, kilometre by kilometre. And when they do get here, they think they've arrived. I want to tell them it's only just begun. Fleeing sits in your blood, it's passed on to your unborn child and like a tumour it grows inside you over time. Everything you've lost, what you think you'll be able to get over, you can't. It's still there. Even the fate you feared, even what you fled. Even your painful, bloody death is still with you. Still there. It moves through your nightmares. It moves through your memories. All those memories of the ones you lost. What you've fled from lives with you as vividly as the strange new life you're trying to adapt to. It won't go away! You are condemned, and your children are too. Everything remains, and everything is passed down.

I decide to go ahead with the radiation after all. There's a large mass in my liver that they want to remove.

I start laughing when Christina tells me.

'If it's in the liver, then it's all over anyway. Will that save me? What's the point?'

She stands at the foot of the bed and shakes her head. 'Nahid, I didn't promise to save you. I can't promise you anything. We just think it might help to radiate the tumor away, that's all.'

She looks down at her papers. We're both silent for a moment. Then she puts her hand on my foot and squeezes it.

'If we don't remove this tumour, Nahid, then it's over. Let us do it.'

And she turns and walks away.

It's getting close to two years since they told me I had six months left to live. Since they told me I was dying. It's like a fog, this time. A fog of cars picking me up at my front door. My body painstakingly leaving my building and climbing into the car. A fog of paramedics. A fog of hospital doors. Doors I step through. Doors I'm rolled through on a stretcher. Doors opened by the doctor. Treatments, test results, collapse. Vomit bucket next to my sofa and carton after carton of meal replacements delivered to my door. They form a tower in the hall. I'm not strong enough to carry them into the apartment. I'm not strong enough to drink or eat. A fog of phone calls from unknown numbers. The doctor, counsellor, dietician. The dietician. It's laughable.

'I needed you more when I was healthy,' I said to her when we first met. 'What can you do for me now?'

She continued calling anyway. They all did. The dietician's calls were the first I opted out of. Then the counsellor. Christina, she called more than she needed to. More than you could expect. So I talked to her. She became my Sonja, my dietician, my doctor and counsellor all in one. A fog of conversations, which began with the words:

'Hi Nahid, it's Christina, how are you today?'

'How are you today?' There is no new answer. I have cancer. It's devouring my body. It will kill me. It's a fog, everything's a fog except for that midsummer day when all was bright and full of life. We managed to create one beautiful memory. We spent so much time in that beautiful archipelago, visited it over so many years, and in the end we made one beautiful memory. One thing that is nothing but beautiful.

I tell myself, I have to live long enough to become a grandmother. I have to see her. I have to tell her she was born free. Tell her she has roots here. That her grandfather lies in this earth, so this is her land. Even if we aren't by her side, we were the ones who made her free. We planted her roots. We did that, Masood and I. I want to say that to her.

So I push the bell. When the nurse comes in, I say: 'I have decided to live.'

She looks at me with her head cocked to the side.

Wondering if I'm hallucinating again or just rambling.

'I mean that I want to start radiation. As soon as possible!'

She nods. Readjusts my blanket.

‘I’ll tell Christina,’ she says. I see that she wants to say something more. That she wants to make sure that I don’t hope too much. I want to stop her, so I close my eyes. Pretending to fall asleep. She stays. Changes the water in my flowers. Throws away juice bottles and wipes off my table. That’s not her job. She does it because she feels sorry for me. I know that. She does it because she knows the radiation won’t make any difference. It can’t do more than buy me days, weeks, a month. But I don’t want the nurse’s compassion. I know that a little time is all I need. I just need to be here until the baby comes.

They keep me at the hospital in anticipation of my new treatment beginning.

'I want you here so I can keep an eye on you,' Christina says.

'I've been here for weeks,' I protest. I really want to go home. But then I realise that I have no idea how long I've actually been in the hospital. I have no idea what day it is. I think about it, but can't remember what month it is. I remember that the baby's due date is in January. Has Christmas come and gone?

I ask Christina, and she looks worried. She starts asking lots of questions.

'Do you know which country you are in, Nahid?'

'I'm not senile, Christina! I'm in Sweden.'

'Do you know what city you were born in?'

I am about to say Stockholm, but it sounds wrong even in my own head. I try to remember, but something stops me. Like a wall between me and my own thoughts.

'Of course I do,' I reply and look away.

'Nahid, what's your daughter's name?'

I stare into the air. Feel the wall becoming thicker and thicker. On my side of the wall there is nothing. Nothing. It is like a vacuum.

I meet Christina's eyes, and I know before she says anything. Before they lift me onto a stretcher and roll me away and push me into the large X-ray machine where I have a claustrophobic panic attack, shouting and screaming until they have to take me out and give me a sedative before they push me back in again.

The cancer is in my brain now. It has built a nest among my memories. Among my thoughts, right before my eyes. It sits like a wall between me and everything I want to say. Everything I was going to say, before I disappear. Everything I can see, the only thing I wanted to see. I am going to disappear, before I can die.

'How long until January?' That is my only question.

'It's only a few weeks, Nahid,' Christina says.

'Will I be here? Will I make it to January?'

'I don't know, Nahid.'

She strokes my hair. Sitting just inches away, but she is fuzzy. Like a blurry photo. I squint to catch her contours.

'Help me make it to January. Please help me to be here in January.'

I see in my fog that her face tightens. That she is holding back.

'Christina. Please, don't do this to me. Please. I'm going to be a grandmother. Let me become a grandmother.'

I hear her crying. I can't see, but I hear. 'It's unfair,' I mumble. 'It's not fair.'

The next morning, I ask the nurse to help me sit up in bed, and for a cup of coffee. I need something bracing. Something that can help me through the fog. I want to ask for tequila. I am craving a shot of tequila and a cigarette. But my fog wouldn't be able to handle that. It strikes me that I will never drink tequila or smoke a cigarette again, and it makes me lose heart for a moment. Not because it is important. But because it is just one more thing. Something else that is being taken from me. Something else that is banal or taken for granted by others, but that I will never experience again.

I have two phone calls to make. Two conversations that I have to take care of while I still have my strength, one to my mother and one to my daughter. The rest can be finished by someone else. I pick up the phone, and weigh it in my hand while trying to decide which one should come first. Then I get stuck there, and it isn't until the nurse comes into the room and stands next to me with a cup of coffee that it comes back to me. I remember what it was I wanted to do.

I call Maryam first. It seemed natural. Dealing with the past before I move on to the future.

She answers after a few rings. It surprises me. They've been trying to avoid my calls lately, my nagging them to let me talk to my mother.

'Nahid, *salam*!' She sounds shrill.

'Nahid, how are you, *aziz*? Are you still in the hospital? When do they start your treatment? Nothing has changed here, Nahid, don't worry. Focus on yourself, on Aram, on the baby, soon the baby will be there, Nahid.'

I hear her words, I do. But I listen to her tone and the background noise, and her short, shallow breaths and the tension quivering in the air between syllables.

'Maryam, I want to talk to Mama,' is all I say. 'I want to talk to Mama.'

I have said those words so many times now. So many times in such a short time, and they've still kept her from me. 'I have news!' I shouted. 'Please, I'm calling to make her happy.' But I wasn't allowed. They haven't let me talk to my mother since her stroke and now I hear it. I hear it and I know it, despite the fog. Despite what I have called to say. I know it and if my heart had a mouth it would howl in pain.

'Maryam, I want my mother. Please, I want my mother.'

My sobs drown out her words. I don't want to hear her words. But in the end I lose my breath and strength, and she says it again.

'*Nahid joon*, my heart. Mama is gone, sweetie. Darling. Mama is gone, my heart. Mama passed on.'

It shouldn't be so painful to lose your mother when you yourself are about to die, die any time now. When you know that your separation won't be long. That this is just a temporary sadness. But it is. I drop the phone on the floor and sink down under the covers, into my fog again. I don't know how long I am away, but I hear voices come and go and I want to tell them my mother is gone. *Please, hold me, because my mother is gone*. But they take my vague sounds for hallucinations. I lift my arm in the air, trying to grab hold of someone, whoever is there. Trying to tell them I am still here.

Aram wants me to come home with them. Live there. She stands in the hospital room talking with Christina and her voice could be mistaken for firm, but I hear only panic.

'I can take care of my own mother. We'll deal with whatever needs to be sorted out.'

Christina tries to protest.

'There is a lot to handle. The morphine, medicines, all the practicalities. She can't walk by herself, she sees very little. And then there are the hallucinations . . . They will get worse and worse as more tumours press on her brain. Those things can be difficult.'

Aram stands with her hands on her waist. That is all I can see. A black figure with a huge belly and hands at her waist. She looks like an angry troll, a fairy-tale creature.

'This is my mother, Christina.'

Her voice breaks, and they both stand in silence for a moment. I remember. Those were the words she said during our first meeting, the first time I was admitted here. There lies the weight of guilt and shame between them. *Why didn't you save my mother, I told you this is my mother, how can you take her away from me?*

'I'll call home care,' Christina says, and leaves the room.

I raise my hand and catch Aram's attention.

'Let me go home to my place. I want to be in my own home.'

I try to talk clearly, and she understands. She takes my hand and kisses my forehead.

'I know you do, Mama. I know. I wish you could.'

She rests her lips against my skin and I feel the warmth and the wetness of her tears. I want to ask why I can't. Why she is crying. I want to ask: What is happening to me? I can't remember.

But my words are gone for the day. I can't find them, and I can't make my mouth form them.

It is the paramedics who come and pick me up. They lift me onto their stretcher and roll me through the hospital, to the emergency entrance. I want to make a joke about it. To say it is surreal. To be delivered home by ambulance, when you're really on your way somewhere else. I want to say so. But the lamps shine too brightly and the machines beep too loudly and I close my eyes instead.

I wake up when they lift me into the car. 'It's my birthday soon.'

I speak.

'I'm turning fifty-five. I've got so old. Come to my party. You have to come to my party.'

I don't think they heard me. I don't even know if I actually said the words. I try to repeat them, but they are lost.

My mother and I went to the cemetery together once. The place where political prisoners were buried. The executed received no funeral. They were just put in the ground. Some families were told. Some even knew where their children's bodies were. Others, like us, just assumed. We assumed this was where she lay. Where she rested. A fourteen-year-old body, that shouldn't need to rest. That wasn't meant to rest.

My mother hadn't said much after that night. She'd gone to the prison. She told us so later. She knew we would have gone in her place, and she feared they would take us, too. She'd gone there and asked for her daughter. They had said that her daughter wasn't there. When she turned to leave the guard shouted after her:

'Shame, *khanom*. What kind of mother doesn't know where her daughter is? What kind of mother has to knock on the prison gate asking for her?'

Mama walked over to him, went up close and stared into his eyes. Then she spat in his face. She knew they could have taken her then and there. It was a miracle they didn't.

But he looked down at the ground, that guard. A boy barely older than Noora. He looked down at the ground, and my mother held on tight to her handbag and walked away as fast as her rheumatism allowed.

And then, two weeks and four days after our Noora disappeared, we were sitting at breakfast, she was pouring tea in my glass, and she said in calm voice:

'Today I want to visit Noora.'

Masood looked up with disbelief and pain in his eyes. 'Mother, do you know something?'

Mama reached across the table for some cheese.

'I know that my girl has left us. My heart knows it.'

Masood started to protest, but she put up her hand and shushed him.

'Today we're going to the cemetery,' she said, firmly and calmly.

Masood turned to me, but I couldn't meet his eyes. So he got up, pulled on his jacket and slammed the front door on his way out. Mama didn't move a muscle. She just sat there. Back straight. Hands in her lap. Her coat and scarf over her chair. Her shoes placed next to the wall and her bag next to them. She was ready. I didn't understand how she managed to be, but she was.

I smiled at her. It took so much for me to bring forth that smile, but I did. I smiled and said:

'We'll do what you want, Mama.'

And so we dressed in our finest clothes, took each other by the hand and walked towards the bus. I wanted to fall down on the ground and never move again. But I held my mother's hand. I smiled when she looked at me, and we sat for the whole of the bus ride holding hands. In her other hand, she had a bundle of carnations. She must have bought them the day before and forgotten to put them in water. They hung over her knees, drooping. I remember thinking: *This is not how it's done. This is wrong.* But what else could we do?

The cemetery was enormous and our walk long. I felt how my mother limped, how her rheumatism tore at her. But her face didn't change, she held herself erect and her face impassive. Once we were among the unmarked graves of the executed she dropped to the ground. It was as if her body, like mine, wanted to sink completely into the earth and finally had permission to do so.

She bent over the yellow sand. I sat down by her. I heard her whisper, and I heard her kiss the ground, again and again. All I could do was lift the sand in my hands and watch it stream back down to earth.

I see my mother. She stands in my room with her arms full of drooping carnations. She has come to me, come to say goodbye. I see her coming towards me, dressed in her black coat with a scarf over her hair. I see the serenity of her face and her firm grip on her handbag. She kneels down next to me. Kisses the floor.

'How did you get here, Mama? Who let you in? How did you get here, Mama? I thought you were gone. I thought it was over. Mama, I have something to tell you. Mama, listen.'

Someone puts a cold hand on my forehead. Shushes me. Sings softly. My vision becomes cloudy, the contours of my mother start to disappear.

'Mama, don't leave me. Stay with me, I need you. I'm going to make it better again! I'll give back what I took. I promise.'

But she's gone. She has left the carnations, brown and rotten.

I feel it in my head when the world snaps into focus and clarity returns. It sounds like a click, like opening a jar of mayonnaise for the first time. A seal being broken.

It clicks and I open my eyes. It is dark and windy outside the large windows. Tree branches tap against the glass. Inside the lights are low. On the dining table candlelight flickers. On the windowsill an Advent candlestick stands, and in the corner a Christmas tree is all lit up. Classical music is playing at a low volume, and I hear voices in the distance. Smell fried meat and creamy potatoes in the oven. I think for a moment I'd imagined it, but it is unmistakable. The click. The clarity.

'Aram.'

My voice is hoarse and rough, and I clear my throat. 'Aram!'

The voices fall silent, but no one comes. It is as if they are listening to see if the cry is repeated. As if they think they might have imagined it.

'Aram!' I cry out with a clear voice now, and hear her drop whatever she has in her hands and run. She comes running, stops in the doorway to the living room where I lie, and stares at me.

'*Salam madar*,' I say. Hello love.

She stands in the doorway with her hands on her lower

back and looks at me with wide eyes and it is as if there is a glow around her. A shimmer of light shining from her face, from her glistening hair held high in a ponytail. From a spot behind her head. She looks like an angel, what I've always imagined an angel might look like. I think, we're so close to each other, the baby and me. I'm close to death and she's close to life, and soon we'll both cross that thin line. Perhaps we are in the same place. I feel safe in that thought. I feel for the first time in such a long time that I'm not alone. I won't die alone. We will meet and hold hands and then push each other gently over the line.

Aram wants my clarity and I want it for myself. She wants answers to her questions. Words that she can live with. But I just want peace and quiet. I just want to lie with my eyes open, staring at the tree branches moving outside the window, and to feel myself a part of that movement, a part of life.

She sits on the edge of the sofa, and the first thing she says is:

'You missed Christmas, Mama.'

It awakens a darkness in me. Her comment, it makes me angry. Who cares about Christmas, who cares if I missed this one when I'm going to miss each one that is to come.

'We missed you,' she says, and that is it. That is what makes me angry. That she wants to have Christmas with me, for her sake. She wants to have one last Christmas, a mental image of me in their Christmas.

'I have a present for you.'

She says it with a firm voice. As if she wants to convince both of us that this is right. That giving me a Christmas present is the right thing to do, the right thing to fill one of our last moments with.

It makes me happy. It is a strange feeling that starts in my stomach and climbs up into my throat and reaches for my lips. I know I smile with my mouth; the rest of my face is rigid. Eyes frozen in a squint. She lifts a big package, and I throw up my arms with force. Take a firm hold. Pull the package close to me. I feel that she is there at the other end, she doesn't dare let the full weight rest on my chest. I feel that we are both somehow grabbing hold of this moment.

'I hope you like it. That you can . . . use it.'

She doesn't know when I will wake up again. If I will. She doesn't know if my clarity will swim out into the universe and disappear into the sea of memories and unfulfilled hopes. She doesn't know if this is my last breath in the harbour, and she knows I don't want to talk. That I don't want to give her what she needs, words of comfort, caresses that will heal, that she can carry with her for the rest of her life. So she gives me something, she gives me something I absolutely don't need and I won't use and it makes us both happier than you'd expect. Happier than we thought we could be.

She tears open the package and the box inside. Quickly, quickly, like it is an emergency. I squint, but I can't see. She tells me what it is. An expensive handbag, the kind I want, but don't think is meant for someone like me. It is an expensive bag, and I am a Marxist, or at least I once was, and it makes me feel like I am worth something. Like I am worth more than I thought.

What I see is the colour. It is red, or some part of it is red, I don't know. I hold it up, and I take her hand.

'It matches my red boots,' I say. 'I can wear them together.'

She squeezes my hand.

'That's a good idea, Mama,' she says. 'We'll take a walk together, with the bag and your red boots.'

I look up and see her, for a second I see her sharply. Her face is as determined as her voice. She isn't going to give in for a second. She is going to keep me alive. She is going to keep me alive as long as we both need it.

I hear their voices in the distance, and it bothers me. They have moved me into the bedroom. I lie in their bed, and I don't know where they are sleeping. I hear them leave and lock the door, and come back with excited voices and bags rustling. I hear them assemble the crib in the living room. I hear their restrained laughter and light footsteps. I hear how she lies on her side on the rug breathing heavily while he finishes. I hear them spinning plans and dreams, and I hear their longing. They are building a place in their home and in their hearts, they are putting together a future with their bare hands while I lie here. Aram comes in to me occasionally. She comes often, I know that she does. But it feels like occasionally. Now and then. She looks over my medications and moistens my lips with cotton wool and strokes my hair. She crosses my threshold and steps from life into death. What soon will pass and what soon will come.

I can't talk. I can't say what I feel, and I feel so much. I feel that this is wrong. I want her to sit by my bed, hold my hand, say goodbye, be with me in this coerced waiting that comprises my whole world. It can wait, the new. The rest. The rest will be there later, I am what will disappear. I feel it is wrong, what she is doing. I wish she wasn't pregnant. Wish she could be mine. Wish she could focus all of her attention here, in my direction.

That she could understand I brought her into this world for me, so I wouldn't be alone, wouldn't end up lying here alone. She owes me that. She is obliged to protect me from loneliness. *You're deserting me!* I want to cry when I hear her folding baby clothes and gently placing them in the drawer. *You will regret this.*

A medical team comes each day. Probably they come several times a day, I don't know. I can smell that it is them. It isn't a bad smell to me, it feels like home. All my hours in hospitals, nursing homes, clinics. All my hours in a white coat, all my hours caring for others. Sometimes I see myself coming towards me. In white, with my hair in a bun and lips bright red. I see myself rise up and take me by the hand. Lift up a hairbrush and stroke my hair with long, gentle movements. Pull up a stool and take pink nail polish out of my pocket. Paint my nails while singing one of my songs. One of the ones I always sang to my patients. I see myself coming towards me and I sing. I am always singing. I wish I could have been my nurse. I wish I could sing my songs. Sometimes, I realise that it is her. In short, sharp moments I see it. How Aram sits with my hands in her lap and paints my nails while she sings. She is always singing.

That day I hear no songs. I smell their scent coming towards me, and I sense them standing over me. They grab hold of me roughly. I can't say anything, I can't ask them to stop. They thrust tubes in my arms and place oxygen over my nose. There are more of them than usual, I can hear it from the closeness between their bodies. They bump into each other and move rapidly. Then they disappear all of a sudden, and that is when I understand. That's when I feel my breath and realise that it is thinning out. Each breath thrusts towards the edges of my lungs and can't find the way out. It rattles and hisses inside me and it feels like I am stuck. Like I am stuck inside myself and can't get out.

They come back and lift me onto a stretcher. I try to turn my head, searching for the outline of Aram. But I know that she isn't in the room. She is standing outside the door, and something is wrong. There are so many of them, and they obscure my view, and I want to shoo them away with my arm but I have no control. I can't lift my arm and I can't open my eyes enough for anyone to understand I am still here. They wheel me through the apartment and out into the hall, where I hear her. She moans. Breathing heavily, rhythmically. They stop for a moment as we pass her. She sits down. Holding her hands on her belly. That is all I can see. She reaches for my hand. She presses it so gently, but so firmly, that I feel life pulsing between us.

'We're coming, Mama. We're coming.'

Her voice is strained. I want to hear more, to understand what is going on. But she bends down and holds back a scream, and then the moment has passed. They wheel me out into the cold stairwell, and I close my eyes.

We're coming. The words spin around in my head, my body, like gargling water in your mouth, around and around and everywhere. *We're coming.*

They sit next to my bed. My mother, in the black dress she wore the day we went to the cemetery. She has her hands on her knees, rocking back and forth, as she did when I came home and she knew it was Noora who had been taken. Maryam, her head bent forward. Her lashes cast long shadows across her face. She has a pencil behind her ear. Her mahogany hair flows over her shoulders. She's beautiful, so beautiful. I know a blue handprint pulses on her cheek. That's why her head is bowed. And behind them, behind them stands Noora. With two braids and a beret. With large glasses and a joyful smile. Fourteen years old, on an adventure. She's the only one who looks at me. Her gaze captures mine, a thousand words. Every word I've longed to say since that day.

I know the smell and know that I'm in hospital again. Movement, bodies. They press on me, attach new tubes. I hear the sound of a pump and I know what it is. I know they're injecting morphine into my body. They want to take away my pain, they want to calm me. Get me to let go and drift away. I try to grab hold of someone by tugging on a sleeve. I try to ask for more time. Just a little more time. I try to scream. I'm not ready, not yet! But my movements aren't visible to their eyes, and my cries are soundless. I can't hold on. I feel myself letting go, letting go. I'm floating away. It's a comfortable feeling, I'm the most comfortable I've been in a long time. It's like lying on a beach, the sun high, a breeze caressing you, and you doze off. Into a state between sleep and wakefulness.

I hear it then. The sound, it seems far away. Far away in time and space. A baby's cry. I try to move, but it's as if my body is sinking into a mud hole. *Mama is here*, I want to say. *Mama is with you. Mama will never leave you.* The words you say to a crying baby. *Mama will never leave you.*

I hear it again. A cry that grabs hold of my numb body. It sounds close now, it sounds like it's approaching. Another cry, and then Aram coming towards me. She's dressed in white, her hair in a knot, her lips red and her arms holding a child. For a moment, it's as if I see myself and then I see my mother coming towards me with a newborn Noora in her arms, but then it clicks and everything becomes clear again.

Aram pulls the chair as close to my bed as she can get.

'Mama,' she says. 'Mama, I'm here. I'm here with you.'

She lifts my arms, doing for me what I can no longer do for myself. She puts them across my chest. Then she says those words. The words I have yearned for, yearned until I thought I'd stopped yearning, stopped hoping.

'She's here now. Noora is here. You did it, Mama.'

She lays the baby on my chest. Just like that. Just like that, she's here. Just like that, she's back. The scent of life overwhelms me. The soft scent of untouched skin, of a new beginning.

I try to bend my neck in order to see her properly. Aram lifts up my head and helps me, helps me to see.

The baby opens her eyes. The baby. Noora. My little Noora.

Her eyes are bright blue. Blue like the sea. Blue like the

archipelago, like the sky above the bridges we drove over, back and forth, around and around. Such beauty. I feel her weight against my chest, on my heart. I imagine my heartbeat pulsing inside her body, giving strength to her being.

'Beloved child. I'm your grandmother, dear one. I'm your grandmother.' I don't know if I actually say the words out loud, but I see that she's listening. 'I was the one who brought you here. It was us.'

*

Their outlines are dissolving, and soon they're gone. The light wanes. My body is heavy in the bed, the weight of the baby is on my chest. I feel Aram holding my hand in hers. I feel it, the weight of the bodies I'm leaving behind. Aram is singing. Her voice follows me into the darkness that receives me. She sings my songs, and inwardly I smile. They will sing our songs, our songs will never die.

To buy any of our books and to find out more about Fleet, our authors and titles, as well as events and book clubs, visit our website

www.littlebrown.co.uk

and follow us on Twitter

@FleetReads
@LittleBrownUK